The Californios

The Californios

LAURAN PAINE

Sagebrush
Large Print Westerns

Library of Congress Cataloging in Publication Data

Paine, Lauran.
  The Californios / Lauran Paine.
    p.   cm.
  ISBN 1-57490-053-6 (hc : alk. paper)
  1. Large type books. I. Title.
[PS3566.A34C28   1996]
813'.54--dc20   96-43606
                                                                         CIP
Cataloguing in Publication Data is available from
the British Library and the National Library of Australia.

Sagebrush Large Print Westerns are published in the United
States and Canada by Thomas T. Beeler, Publisher, Box 659,
Hampton Falls, New Hampshire 03844-0659.
ISBN 1-57490-053-6

Published in the United Kingdom, Eire, and the Republic of
South Africa by Isis Publishing Ltd, 7 Centremead, Osney
Mead, Oxford OX2 0ES England. ISBN 0-7531-5502-8

Published in Australia and New Zealand by Australian Large
Print Audio & Video Pty Ltd, 17 Mohr Street, Tullamarine,
Victoria, 3043, Australia. ISBN 1-86340-684-0

Manufactured in the United States of America

The Californios

CHAPTER 1

JOHN MARTIN SAT BACK AGAINST THE CRACKED LEATHER cushion of the surrey beneath the gay, rippling fringe of the edging, watching the familiar land unroll around him. He had his strong hands lying together in his lap, one cluster of fingers gripping the other fist with slight force. He felt a thrill of emotion, thinking ahead to the next stop. There was a sense of satisfaction within him—if not peace. The authorities had granted his petition for a rancho. It still amazed him that no land grant could be reckoned in less than a league. To John Martin, a Spanish league was still an endless eternity of land, in his head. He marveled that these great people, in their Utopia of fertile riches, were so grandly extravagant and casually generous; as though the bounty of Heaven was theirs to dispense.

A Spanish league was roughly four thousand, four hundred and twenty-eight acres. More, actually, but that was still more than he could conceive of. And yet—they had approved his request for four leagues. Seventeen thousand, seven hundred and fourteen acres. It was a staggering, incredible amount of land to a man who had never owned so much as an acre before. And all for nothing. Just because of a friendship with old Augustin Perez.

Above his head the little fringe vibrated nervously, as though in accompaniment with his restless spirit. His nostrils were flared against the outward rush of his breath and his profile, as it held steady, drinking in the pastoral endlessness of California's fabulous inland valley, was clear cut and bronzed. Handsome, like a copper medallion.

He was coming home now. Established in the soil of his

1

adoption. More than an outsider, because he had taken the oath of allegiance and citizenship; a requisite for the land. John Martin was now and henceforth, a Mexican subject. If not by birth and breeding, at least by law and his own given word. Even the grant was listed as the property of Juan Martin. His last name, a common one in the Mexican and Spanish territories, would now be pronounced correctly, where before, the Californian pronunciation had been incorrect for an English name. Marteen, now, properly, Juan Marteen.

He knew that the next long, undulating roll of the coastal road would show him the little sun-baked village of Santa Barbara again. Shaded, squatty, none too clean perhaps, but always pleasant and smiling and honest.

He loved it. In spite of the uneasiness that was beginning to tincture the air farther south, and perhaps even northward, toward Monterey and Yerba Buena; here, in his own village, as it had been for hundreds of years there was still the peace, even laziness and indifference that made it so pleasant to him. This, because Juan Martin was a man who had lived recklessly, brutally, on the other side of this turbulent continent.

It was sitting like that, tense and with a soft shade of a smile at the far corners of his mouth, that Elena Gardia saw him from where she sat beside her aging, handsome husband. She studied the lean, sun-darkened face with its startling gray eyes and aura of savagery, from beneath long and tantalizingly upcurving eyelashes. Her glances were surreptitious at first, then again defiant of propriety, which was no part of her nature anyway, she would stare openly at him letting the thick-waisted passengers' wives think what they might.

Francisco Gardia saw his wife's glances at the

younger man. He was a formidable hacendado, although twenty years and more his wife's senior. Wealthy in cattle and horses and measureless leagues of land that were held under the name of his ancient family, Francisco was a physical bull with prodigious, almost legendary strength and a jealous nature that had left a trail of personal wars behind him through a stormy life. But he saw these glances of his young wife with a sense of misgiving, too, for Francisco Gardia's blood was slowing; running less heatedly through leathery veins. It made him, if not resigned, certainly less vitriolic and impulsive than he had been before. A little tired, even, of the incessant assaults life still launched against his increasing desire for peace and harmony.

Francisco appraised the younger man. He saw a sturdy Americano dressed in the attire of a native ranchero. An adopted one, no doubt. A man with a flash of steel in him. One of that increasing brotherhood that was making the Mexican officials uneasy and fearful. He looked down at the hands, saw them holding together tightly, glanced up again into the face and read tension there, too, and wondered. These newcomers, they were always too eager; so tense and vital and direct.

Francisco shrugged. The movement brushed his thick shoulder against Elena's arm and he saw the black eyes swinging around looking up into his face in question. He turned away, letting the countryside absorb him. There was no reason to let her see what he couldn't erase in a second. Weariness and melancholy, fused with something that was becoming to look more and more like resignation, on the handsome face of her husband.

When the surrey stopped at Santa Barbara they all got

3

down. Juan Martin saw the venomous, outraged look the massive Doña Martinez, of Rancho Soledad, shot at the voluptuous Gardia woman and was surprised by it. He had no time for reflection though, because Hernando Vaz was feeling for his arms with a great smile that creased his boyish features into a gargoyle's grimace, then strong arms were pounding him sturdily on the back and little Carmen, Hernando's companion, was showing happiness at his safe return just as enthusiastically if less boisterously, by flashing magnificent teeth and glowing black eyes that went through his heart.

"It was a success, then amigo," Hernando said between constricting embraces that made breathing hazardous and difficult.

Juan pushed back with a laugh and a shake of his head. "How did you know?"

Vaz wagged his head triumphantly, putting both hands on his hips. "It was ordained—but no—not only that, for the picture is plain on your face."

"Si, it was approved. I have my rancho. The full four leagues of it." He canted his head wryly, still smiling at a joke they were all enjoying, and told the rest of the joke, which was on himself. "Of course, there were the pitfalls Augustin mentioned."

"El Mordida?" Hernando asked dryly.

"Yes, 'The bite'."

"How much did the dogs nick you for, then?"

Juan shrugged. He had come to talk as much with his motions as with his mouth, after the custom of the Californians. "It was small, Hernan'. I'll survive."

Carmen ventured closer now that the bearish scuffling was over and the danger of being inadvertently trampled had passed.

4

"Juan—you got the citizenship as well?"

Juan nodded without answering, knowing how this interested her equally as much as his acquisition of the land that adjoined her grandfather's rancho.

"You see before you, one Juan Martin, a loyal and avowed citizen of Mexico."

Hernando Vaz turned to the girl with an impatient look. "Carmencita, you are around those old ones too much. Their talk of trouble is so much wind in the treetops."

Juan regarded Vaz strangely, saying nothing, but Carmen matched his slight frown with a dazzling smile, being silent because she wouldn't have to speak to him. She never had to. Hernando relented immediately; it was his nature to be passionate in all things. A short laugh signaled the passing of the small storm. The girl's face was radiant and happy when she spoke.

"Señors—we'll have a celebration, a fiesta. It'll fit in nicely with the matanza, don't you agree?"

Vaz threw a beaming look at Juan. It said how wonderfully clever little Carmen was; so versatile and understanding, and, naturally, lovely also.

"Juan—you should acquire this little imbecile. She has the sainted ability to see into the future and plan for it." Hernando's eyes were alight. "Of course we'll have a celebration. Augustin will want this to happen. Old bones live for little else—that, and grandchildren, of course," he added with a sly, teasing look at the girl. She didn't blush. There could be little shock between two who had grown up as brother and sister.

Juan saw Elena Gardia lingering beside the handsome buggy of her husband, looking back at the three of them. He noticed that the beautiful girl had a parasol—one of those dainty, frilly things the rancheros got from the

5

Boston brigs that came along infrequently for the coastal trade in hides and tallow. He lowered his glance from the girl and saw Carmen looking intently up at him.

"Juan—you know who she is, do you not?"

"No," he said quietly, risking another glance and seeing the buggy start away with the mighty bulk of Francisco making it lean awkwardly on one side. "If I did, I'm sure I'd remember it through."

Carmen noticed his second glance, too. "That is Elena Gardia of Rancho San Buenaventura. She's a vixen!"

"Ha!" Hernando interrupted scornfully "They're all she-foxes, amigo. It is just that some are worse than others, is all. That one," his face showed a strange intentness, "is the most beautiful of them all—that's the difference. And old Francisco—he's killed his share of hombres, too, in his time—grows too old and heavy, I think. There will be a day when he regrets marrying one so young and full of fire."

"Hernando!"

He shrugged broad shoulders and smiled queerly at Carmen. "It's the truth, little one, and you know it. She has the vivaciousness of ten women, and that old bull of a husband. What would you, for the love of God? A lie? No; Juan should be warned, of course—that's what's in your mind, for I know you that well—but not frightened away. He is a man, also, Carmen, and a young and unmarried one."

Carmen's eyes were angry now. There was the appearance of master and brute between them when she stamped her foot at him. Juan brought his eyes back from the disappearing buggy in time to avoid a torrent of abuse that wouldn't have injured Hernan' a bit, but would have upset Carmen.

6

"Come, amigos, let's take this good fight to the Rancho San Diego Del Carmelo. It's cooler there and a far more comfortable place to battle."

Old Augustin met them when they rode up. His flood of welcoming words rolled on in a scratchy voice that wasn't silenced until they had returned embraces. Then, because Hernando Vaz was tired of the repetitions in the Old Tongue of formal use for which he had no use anyway, he squeezed Carmen's grandfather very tightly, and the old man was left gasping as he hobbled on the girl's arm, ahead of them to the patio where wine was brought and they settled into the shade and repose of the place.

Augustin Perez was wispy and dehydrated with age. His face was the seamed, sere outline of California's inland valley in the summertime; old out of mind, scarred and indented and patient, with a hope and prayerfulness that was almost childish. His mind was clear and frank and wise, but, like all of the old Colonizers who had been shut away in this dreamy land for so long, apart from the rest of the world, he was naive and easily believing. Typical of the many who fell without quite ever knowing they were being swept away, when the years after '46 stalked by their blighted, ruthless march toward a malignant Destiny.

"You saw Don Pio, then, Juan?"

"Si, Señor. Exactly as you and I planned, right here in this patio. The grant is mine."

"Ah," Augustin said slowly, contentedly. "God wished it."

Hernando was restless. He winked wickedly at Carmen and reaped a quick frown, sank lower on his bench and regarded the huge, awkward spurs on his heels without seeing them.

The girl's eyes were alight when she looked at her

7

grandfather. "You have planned a celebration, perhaps, for Juan's good fortune?"

Augustin inclined his head matter-of-factly. "That—little shadow—has been attended to. Did you think an old man incapable of recognizing the needs—and graces—of our race, then?"

Carmen shook her head, stealing a glance at Hernando, seeing his heavy lids growing heavier after the wine and the coolness of their relaxation, and turned toward Juan.

"Caballero, you have plans for this rancho of yours?"

He smiled at her and winked solemnly at old Augustin. "I have dreams, not plans. They include horses and cattle, and in time—perhaps a wife and all that goes with one."

Austin poured more wine into their glasses. "The house is to be where we discussed it, Juan?"

"Exactly."

Augustin sighed audibly in relief and shot a triumphant glance at Carmen. "It is well, son. An old man is subject to anxieties, but young men are subject to changes of mind."

"Oh?" Juan said, wonderingly.

"Si—it is because I have laborers over there, on that oak knoll we spoke of. They have been making adobes for the past ten days. For this, I have prayed you hadn't changed your mind."

"Señor—!"

"Mother of God!" Augustin exploded quickly, interrupting and gesturing with both hands at once and letting his tufted white eyebrows race wildly upwards in the copper of his coloring. "Is it a sin, then, to help one's neighbors? Am I—an old man—to be denied the pleasures left to my old age? Juan Martin—you

8

wouldn't deny an old one—surely?"

Juan laughed in spite of himself. They were so amazingly innocent, even the old ones. So wonderfully bountiful and generous. To the Californio, there was no such thing as a favor. You had but to talk to one and he immediately and eternally placed himself under your obligation. It was as though he wanted, not only to help you, but guide and establish you as well, and, incredibly enough to the Yankee, he enjoyed every minute of it. Augustin was no exception.

"Well," Juan said dryly. "I can't always lean on Rancho San Diego Del Carmelo."

Augustin brushed this aside with an imperious hand. His face showed clearly that it was a thing beneath consideration; a triviality.

"Tell me, then, Juan; what is the news from the pueblo?" Augustin, like many others, considered Neustra Señora La Reina de Los Angeles, which was becoming another American frontier town with brothels, gunfights and savagery rampant night and day, like they would a dishonored friend. A thing to be alluded to indirectly, not by name.

"Well," Juan said reluctantly. "There is much talk of Fremont and Castro and Pico, of course."

"Seguro. What of them?"

Juan sighed, looked enviously at the slumbering, sprawled form of Hernando. "Pico and Castro are at daggers points, still. But there are other things that have happened."

"Ah?" Augustin said, leaning forward. "What then?"

"Well, General Castro sent a requisition to General Vallejo for horses to be used in making his demonstration against Pio Pico."

"It has become this serious, then?" Augustin asked,

anxiously.

Carmen broke in, sensing more to come. "Patience, grandfather."

Juan was looking down at his hands when he spoke. "These horses were being driven south by Castro's men. His secretary, Arce, was in charge. There were also eight or nine soldiers with them. On the tenth of June, so gossip has it, Arce was surprised on the Cosumnes by a band of Fremont's—irregulars—"

"Bandidos!" Augustin exploded with such violence that it awakened Hernando.

"Bandits, then," Juan continued solemnly, "and the horses were taken away."

"Stolen!" Augustin erupted, his black eyes flashing a savage fire. "And what of the herders? They were put to the sword undoubtedly—Holy Mary!"

"No," Juan said quickly, seeing his host's vivid coloring. "They were released and sent on their way. Castro issued a proclamation saying these men are highwaymen, and calling on the people to take up arms."

Augustin sat rigid, his ancient, thin blood racing in shriveled old veins. "This is terrible news, Juan," he said after the moment it took to regain his composure. "There will be a war—by the Cross. What happened then—afterward?"

Juan looked up and saw Hernando Vaz' eyes, black and bored, on his face. It made him uncomfortable. He didn't glance at Carmen at all.

"Pico and Castro are both crying for retaliation. They seem to have become more or less united against this new enemy."

Hernando's dry tones came from his corner of the patio. "It is well that something has gotten those two old

10

stallions to pull together for a change."

"One moment, Hernando," Augustin said impatiently, still sitting forward. "Juan—did you take the oath of allegiance?"

Juan looked up with a nod. There was a hard, whimsical look around his mouth. It had been bothering him a little since he had done it, too. At the time, in spite of rumors, it had been a small price to pay for his rancho. Now, however, it was beginning to look a little more formidable. Something mute and immense and unrelenting that had set him adrift completely. With the gathering storm clouds, it even made him think of himself as a special kind of a traitor.

Augustin leaned back and made a cigarette with delicate, thin-veined fingers. "This Fremont is a pig! Ha! To some of our Americanos he is a hero and an invader. Does an invader come in rags and flee when horsemen ride round his little mountain top dragging brush behind their horses? Does an invader come sneaking in and murder old men, like this Kit Carson did at Yerba Buena, because he is afraid of his own shadow? No! This Fremont is a man struggling to become a hero, yet without the heart one must have for that role. An illegitimate even, they tell me."

Carmen raised her eyebrows at her grandfather, who shrugged away the niceties with an eloquence that said, plainly enough, this was no time for them.

"When these men come to California, are they not extended our hospitality? Our homes and horses and freedoms? But of course they are. How do they repay us? Like this!" He gestured angrily with the hand holding the little cigarette.

"They are brigands and outlaws, nothing more. Their country has neither declared war against us, nor

11

authorized them to do so. Then—they aren't heroes at all. Just bandits. Am I not right, Juan?"

Juan was acutely conscious that Augustin was probing him. Feeling for the exact depths of his loyalty as a Mexican citizen. A loyal—or disloyal—Californio. He nodded again. "It would seem so," he said, without looking at Augustin. There was so much more to tell. How this same Fremont, with an army consisting of absolutely nothing but rabble—a wanted murderer among them, in fact—had fallen on the sleepy little town of Sonoma, made Mariano Vallejo their prisoner, made a ridiculous little flag from a discarded petticoat and the chemise of a—well—questionable 'lady,' declaring that California was now a sovereign state, independent of Mexico. The maker of this preposterous flag was one William Todd, a nephew of Mrs. Abraham Lincoln.

But Juan mentioned none of this. What good would it serve? Arouse an old man? Perhaps frighten a pretty girl and maybe excite Hernando as well. For what? Por nada. The rancho was distant and isolated, let the mad world whirl wildly beyond, outside of this comfortable vacuum.

It was all rumor and Juan knew it was; still, there were the distinguishable little grains of truth that he recognized, too. The more he thought of it, the more his new allegiance troubled him.

It was Carmen who broke the gloom. She went over to Augustin and laid a small hand on the wiry, withered old arm. "God protects the righteous, Grandfather. We'll have the matanza and fiesta anyway."

"Does he?" Hernando asked wryly.

The near-blasphemy jolted devout old Augustin Perez. He shot a warm glance at this orphaned son of

12

long dead friends.

Again Carmen stepped in with her ability to smooth out the roughness. "Is not the matanza slated for another week ahead?" Augustin nodded, hidden from the warning glare she darted at Hernando. "Good. I'll take care of what you have not gotten around to then." She squeezed the old arm and jerked her head at the younger men, over her grandfather's head. They arose, paid their departing respects and left, walking through the cool house behind her small, full figure.

Outside, Carmen stopped and turned back to face them both. Her eyes were on Juan's face. "Is it—so bad then, our Juan?"

He shrugged, looking over at Hernando. "Quien sabe, Carmencita? Who knows? It will be worse before it gets better, I'm afraid."

Hernando nodded, looking down. "It is just so, friends. Worse before better. But hold you a moment, Juan. Don't you think this Fremont a fool?"

"Worse than that," Juan said savagely. "If he wants to be a Napoleon, why, then, can't he go somewhere else and conquer his empire! We neither need him nor want him, the—"

"Peace, Juan Martin!" She wrinkled her nose at him. "It is as bad to think it as to say it."

He smiled at her. "Well—not quite, Carmen."

She responded to his smile with a shrug. "Well—leave this other to me. Grandfather has forgotten everything but his old friends and the wine. I'll see to the rest of it."

"She will, too," Hernando avowed stoutly, looking his pride of her. "But tell us, then, when the grand fiesta is to be?"

"After Mass—next Sunday; until the food is gone and

13

the feet are numb from dancing."

"The matanza will commence Monday—conceivably?" Hernando was teasing her. They all knew that no celebration—not even a wake—was over so quickly.

Carmen darted him a wicked smile. "For you, perhaps, who grows thick in the middle, but not for me—or Juan, here."

Hernando laughed. He threw his head back to do it, like he always did. "Be sure then, since you want much dancing, to invite Elena Gardia, for there is one who would rather dance than watch her old husband grow richer." He rolled his head sideways at Juan. "And remember what I said. Here is a single man who too, can dance."

"You," Carmen said with fire. "Were built with the soul of a pig."

Hernando was ready, though. "Pray then, little sister, that I do not develop the appetites as well, for Elena Gardia is one to inspire such a—"

"Quiet your mouth!" The black eyes were flashing a steady, scornful fire. "If you have the appetite to match this soul of a pig—and Don Francisco discovers it—he'll pour molten lead into your ears and you'll have no need for Elena Gardia, or any other like her!"

Juan was shocked, and wanted mightily to laugh too. He looked at the small, perfect oval of Carmen's face, and lower, to the symmetry of her figure, so lithe and wholesome. She turned self-consciously and caught him staring at her, blushed and turned away from them.

"Pardon me, Don Juan. Adios, vaqueros." Then she was gone.

Hernando walked beside Juan to their horses. He was thoughtful all of a sudden, the teasing look was gone

14

and in its place was a pensive sort of bewilderment that didn't fit the good-natured, clear face at all.

When they were mounted and riding across the vast acres of the land, he spoke of the things that were on his mind. "Juan, what was there that you didn't tell Don Augustin?"

"Things that would have fired him up like a stove." He then related them to his companion exactly as he had heard them in Los Angeles. Hernando listened in silence, letting his gaze wander over the new growth that was springing up in the near distance, where Augustin's Indians were laying out the hacienda of Juan Martin's rancho. They rode in close to the gnarled oaks where a shop was already half formed, and dismounted.

Not until then did Hernando speak. "Well—isn't it true that Vallejo himself, wants annexation with the United States?"

"I've heard so," Juan said. "But there are the other things to consider, Hernan'."

"Vallejo is a brilliant man, amigo," Hernando said quietly, watching with half his interest, the laborers putting great beams in the shop building. "So—if he's satisfied that such an alliance will be good for us, should we question it?"

"Hernan'," Juan said impatiently. "There is the difference in temperament of these people, here, and the Americanos. Do you want all this changed?" He waved a hand dramatically, without meaning it to be so, over what was now his land. "They will change it. I know. I've seen them take over new lands before."

Hernando's eyes squinted at Juan. "You talk like a born Californian. Shouldn't we want progress?'"

Juan hated the word. That was why he had journeyed to this far land, embraced it and lost himself within its pastoral borders.

"Progress! Hernan', there is no way to improve on perfection. We Californians have such perfection here. Do you want to work harder, live less, worry more and die younger—for this purpose?"

"You have given this much thought, I see."

"But of course. It's our future, Hernan'."

"You sound like Augustin. Listen, amigo, forget it." The dark eyes narrowed again. "This Elena Gardia, for example—she's more interesting than these madmen. Let me tell you of her. Here, sit down," he dropped quickly, Juan less so. He was still stiff from the journey. "But—before that, old friend, let's talk of this—your rancho. It's going to be wonderful, Juan. I envy you. Still—someday—"

"Someday," Juan finished for him. "You'll be the lord of one as good and probably much better, amigo."

"True," Hernando said without a single hint of boasting. "Now, this Elena Gardia—ah—what a handsome, most beautiful woman she is, by the Cross, Juan. She had two lovers, once. Francisco found them out. He killed them. She is one designed to drive men into the dampest of graves willingly." Hernando smiled with a near look of sincerity in his eyes, too.

Juan grunted and stretched out under the tree, watching the flawlessness of Heaven, feeling the inner peace of a landed man, yet knowing that somewhere, buried beneath this pleasant solstice of emotions and comfort, was uneasiness as well.

"Go on, Hernan', tell me of this 'yegua,' as you call her." He thought of little Carmen and grinned. "But you'd better be careful of your thoughts at Rancho San Diego Del Carmelo. What Carmen doesn't like, she makes no secret of."

16

"Well," Hernando said earnestly. "There are so few like Elena Gardia. She sets a man afire. There is this old saying, old youngster. 'En el pais de las ciegos, el tuerto es rey'!"

"Certainly," Juan said drowsily. "I understand. 'In the land of the blind, the one eyed is king'. How do you mean it vaquero?"

"Like this. Carmen is beautiful, we both concede this. There are many beautiful women around us. But Elena Gardia, who is not only beautiful but wonderful as well and interested. She has all the things, the secrets and the knowledge, that these others do not have. Surely, it is impossible that either of us could marry her—if we would—for she is, of course, Francisco's property. But think you closely of the madness of such an alliance, a lifetime, then, with her. As God is my witness. Juan, she could kill a man, take him over and, by the Cross, make such a wife as few ever have—then throw his carcass aside—and there are few of us who would not let her do it; even be glad to die afterwards."

Juan was listening, but he had to fight sleep to do it. The exertions of the trip and the homecoming were like drugs; too, the warmth of the ground and the hot sun overhead, sapped him.

"But why do you think she would do all this? Where is the proof, dreamer?"

Hernando snorted. "Two graves are the proof. Both of those vaqueros let Francisco kill them. *Let him,* amigo. Isn't that enough proof for those with eyes? Seguro! But she is a witch; there is—God beside me!—a pact with the devil between she and Satan. You'll see for yourself, the way she dances. It can't be otherwise."

Juan, drowsy as he was, could hear the fascination in Hernan's voice. "Listen, vaquero, approach no nearer

17

with this dream of yours. There could be a sea of sorrow ahead for you—and this witch."

Hernando lay back, overcome with the lassitude of the day, the atmosphere. He sighed mightily through parted lips. "I know. I know. Still, there is the attraction of evil, too, one must confess." He heard the even, rhythmic breathing of Juan Martin and spoke softly aloud, but to himself, he thought, and the sky.

"There are many a man could love who would be better for him. Many who would be warm and lovely and lovable, but this Elena Gardia, she is a woman no man could resist." He stirred restlessly. "San Iago! Why is man made thus!"

CHAPTER 2

THE RANCHO SAN DIEGO DEL CARMELO WAS A RIOT OF colorful people, gay caballeros arriving each second on their splendid horses, calling out to one another in exuberant good spirits and echoing the musical laughter of everyone attending the fiesta.

Juan Martin was everywhere plucked on the sleeve by beautiful women and handsome, swarthy men. Their dress was elaborate and vivid; gold and silver thread sparkling lavishly through the less quiet reds and purples and snow whites.

Light was thrown back into the great old rooms from the whitewashed walls decorated with their religious symbols, old, rusty weapons, and hoary tools of the hacendados trade.

Carmen caught Juan's arm and tugged him into a small, shadowy corner. "Juan—you are a handsome Don. Mira! It's those gray eyes. They love you, too, these people. For that I am grateful."

He felt the uneven, lurching stumble inside of him, where his heart lay imprisoned in its cavern. She was always beautiful but now, if possible, even more so.

"Carmen—what can a debtor say? That he is grateful? That's not enough." The gray eyes held her pinioned for a second, then, "That he is thankful for such friends, such a land and such a woman as you, is still not enough." He saw the sudden, uncertain, startled look moving in the background of her eyes and knew instantly it was hopefulness. He regretted what he had said to inspire that look, immediately, and forced up the old impassiveness with its attendant friendliness that he had worn so long.

"It's wonderful, Carmen . . ." It died there. They were looking at one another. He in shame and regret and uneasiness, for he saw the hopeful look widen in her eyes, linger and grow and become something tangible; something she was encouraging to grow from an astonished suspicion to a solid realization. He was angry at himself for under-estimating her perception, and recalled how many times Hernando Vaz had pointed it out to him. She had created all this in a fleeting second, and now the doubt was no longer uncertainty. Feeling miserable, Juan made a slight motion with his head.

"Carmen—I'm worse than a fool. Forgive me." Then he moved quickly away, leaving her alone in the isolation of her corner, looking after him where he was swallowed up in the crowd of guests who beat him on the back and drank toasts to him and indulged in the merciless humor of the Californios.

The California fandango was a hybrid affair that had become perverted from its original source, the Spanish dance. The music, however, was irresistible and blood stirring. Juan danced with eyes that shone their enjoyment. Perspiration came over his body and the great racket carried his laughter to the low ceilings. Once, Hernando Vaz floated by; they exchanged owlish winks and Juan refused to look down at Carmen; not until he was certain they were lost in the crowd, then he shot a quick stare after them and felt his glance drawn down into the ebony eyes of the girl.

She was looking back at him without blinking. With a sober, stony expression on her face. He pulled his glance away quickly, looking up at his partner. The shock was just as abrupt then, too, for Elena Gardia was smiling at him, an abandoned, wicked gleam in her own eyes. She made a slight, mocking bow which he returned automatically, then she spoke, wishing him a good afternoon and complimenting him on the good fortune he had had in acquiring his rancho.

"I knew it was something like this, when I saw you on the surrey from Los Angeles."

He smiled at her. There was sincere appreciation in his glance. She was indeed, as Hernando had said. 'designed to drive men into the dampest of graves'.

She didn't allow his reserve to stand between them, though. "Isn't it your rancho that is being built above San Diego Del Carmelo? Where the hacienda is going up on the little knoll among the oaks?"

"Si, Señora."

"Is it permissible for neighbors to come and watch, Señor?"

"But of course, although San Buenaventura is quite a ways off. The place isn't fit for much in the way of entertaining yet, Señora but of course, when it is, I'll enjoy having the Gardia's as my guests."

Elena laughed and flashed him an appreciative wink.

20

"Yanqui—you are clever; I like that. Come—let's rest a while." She went past him, lightly touching his arm in a dainty command that he obeyed reluctantly, knowing many eyes were on them.

There was some relief, however, when Elena went over where Francisco's burly body was eased onto a bench, and sat down beside her husband, introducing Juan Martin.

Francisco's level eyes were grave and not unpleasant when they bowed to each other. "Augustin has told me of your trip to the pueblo." Juan was also pleased to discuss the rumors he had heard. He was conscious of Elena's eyes on him as he talked.

Francisco's head nodded once in a while, but his glance was on the floor in front of them. Finally he raised his head and looked straight at Juan.

"And you, amigo; where are your sentiments?"

"I am a Mexican subject, Señor."

"Si, of course," the big man answered slowly. "It is always thus, I think, until storm clouds gather. I have known Yanqui Californians before, Señor." He didn't finish, just let it lie there between them.

Juan felt the gentle brush of disparagement across his feelings and colored a little. "Undoubtedly, then, there are also Spaniards, Señor, who have proven false to their born allegiance, too."

Francisco turned on a wry smile. He was a handsome man with laughter wrinkles around his eyes that were grown dim with the passing of the years and less to inspire humor in them, now.

"Of course. You refer to Mariano Vallejo. Well—amigo—it is hard to define one's loyalties at a time like this. There are many things to consider. Mexico holds we Californians by the loosest of bonds. In fact, Señor,

21

we are Spaniards—not Mexicans. The question, then, is whether we should remain Mexicans by law, *and* Spaniards by blood—or become Americans by default."

"Default, Señor?"

"Yes, default. If we don't fight off this—this Fremont and his—essilladores de caballos agenos!—it will be because we are too undecided in our loyalties. Too divided. You must know then, Señor, that a Californio is not a Mexican, and therefore reluctant to die for Mexico; but—in this instance I assure you, if we do not die for Mexico, then we must eventually become the property of the United States. We certainly cannot stand alone. Is it not this simple, in your mind, Señor?"

"Yes," Juan agreed. "I see it much this way."

"Well, then, amigo—you have seen both sides. What would you?"

Juan shrugged, looking into the soft black eyes with their overlay of melancholy. "I do not know, Señor. I am a Mexican by oath of allegiance."

"Caramba, vaquero!" Francisco said with scorn. "That is lip service and nothing more. You are a Californio—not a Mexican, which is to be a—a mataperro—at heart."

Juan smiled ironically. "Señor, you, yourself, are now sowing the seeds of revolt in my breast. So shortly, too, after you asked where my loyalties lay. Can there be *any* loyalty, then, among us?"

Francisco Gardia sighed aloud, looked at Elena, shrugged and watched the dancers swing by morosely. "That is what I mean, Señor. Either a dead Mexican or a vassal American—by default. Ah, God! What will be the outcome?"

Juan caught Elena's steady glance, read the meaning in it and flushed, looking quickly back at her husband.

"I have only two desires, Señor. One, that this Fremont and his—as you called them, 'saddlers of other people's horses'—his rabble army of cut-throats, would go somewhere else to carve out their empire. And two, that life may always remain as it is, here in California." He arose as he finished speaking, looking down at Gardia.

The big ranchero smiled saturninely. "But naturally. Those are the wishes of all of us. Still they change nothing, Señor." He was looking earnestly into Juan's face. "Californians are children; they have always been so. I predict then, that we will lose our identities by default." He raised one mighty arm and tapped with his fingers on Juan's sleeve. "But my own mind is made up, Señor. We will fight them—we will have to. When this happens, I assure you, Francisco Gardia will ride against the United States!"

Juan was struck with the sadness and determination in the man's eyes. He knew, in his heart, as Francisco Gardia must have suspected also, that such a cause was a lost one. The tide of empire was spinning over from the distant cauldron, running down over the continent in a brawling, seething wave of destiny that must eventually fetch up against the Pacific Ocean. It could go no farther without being drowned, so it must end in California, usurping there as it always had before; sweeping the Californio and his way of life forever from this earth.

Juan knew this while he looked into Gardia's face, but there was the oath of allegiance, too. Juan Martin was as hard as steel, but he was no opportunist. He wasn't brilliant enough for that. He inclined his head soberly, slightly.

"When that time comes, Señor," he said quietly, "we may ride together."

Gardia was astonished and showed it. His fine

23

features brightened in amazement and froze that way. Some of the old reckless laughter showed for a moment in the black eyes. He was, for that second, twenty years younger, then he laughed his pleasure and reached out, taking both of Juan's arms and squeezing them.

"San Iago y California, compatriota!"

Juan nodded without Gardia's enthusiasm.

Elena rose swiftly, looking at them both. "There is a new dance starting, Señors." Her eyes were on Juan's face expectantly. He looked at her, then deferred with a bow toward Francisco, but the hacendado smiled ruefully with a careless notion of one hand. "I am too sober for that."

Elena went ahead, Juan following. They took their places, he conscious of the many eyes that swept over them openly and knowingly, she radiant as only a woman on a trail of conquest can be. They danced. Elena made it a point to brush against him when the chances of such a touch were propitious. Juan's perspiration returned, only now it was a nervous sweat. He danced with an almost glum look and she chided him for it.

"What ails you, Don Juan? This is a grand celebration, not a funeral."

"Well," he said tartly, feeling the dampness of his blouse under the short jacket with its heavy embroidery. "I have danced when there was less of an undercurrent to it, Señora."

"Ha! Have you? Then, vaquero, you must take me outside to the barbecue pits, for I am very ravenous."

They went out into the sunset, where the ancient tapestry of the sky was riddled with myriad holes that let starlight shine through. She turned to him before they got near the noisy, crowded pits. "Juan, I'm coming to

24

your knoll tomorrow night."

Astonishment gripped him. "No, that is madness. I don't want you there, Señora!"

She smiled up into his face. The last bloody rays of light fell over them. There was a subtle, macabre aura to the spell. "But I'll come anyway. You have much to learn, vaquero. Elena Gardia can teach you. Listen to me; do you not see there is torture in a woman being married to so old a man?"

He frowned at her. "You listen to me! Life is comfortable now; it wouldn't be—after that." Regardless of the crowning insult of his action, he turned abruptly and walked back toward the house. Elena's black eyes grew shades darker. There was a fury in them that was almost a madness. She turned and went toward the barbecue pits where the raucous bedlam held one voice she knew above the rest. It was the rambling, resonant bass that came from a thick chest and a cheerful throat. Hernando Vaz's voice.

Juan entered the house and was buttonholed almost immediately by ruddy-complexioned Augustin Perez. The old Colonizer was suffused with a sparkling glow that came, without doubt, from his own excellent Madeira.

"Come Juan—on the patio there are gentlemen who would have you join them."

Still angry, Juan followed, threading his way among the people, stopping where it couldn't be avoided, bowing low and returning courtesies.

The first man he saw was Francisco Gardia. The great ranchero was usually the first seen in any room, no matter how filled with other men, because of his vast heft. The resignation was gone from the dark eyes and a latent, rusty fire was flashing out at the fifteen or twenty men who lounged around, holding glasses of Augustin's

25

good wine. Unobtrusively, Juan sought a bench and eased onto it.

Gardia's fist was clenched in front of him. "Caballeros! Something has come to me tonight, in the midst of our troubles. As God knows, and you as well California has suffered much at the hands of Mexico. We have their dungeon soldiers to patrol us, their bandits to tax us and their indifference and distance to make us helpless. Well then—we are now being left entirely to our own resources to handle this Yanqui Fremont, and I say, regardless of Pico and Castro and their interminable squabblings—I say, then, caballeros, we must unite and set the wheels in motion to expel these animals who do not keep their words; who steal our horses and belittle our people!"

Augustin Perez, his eyes shining like two wet olives, nodded emphatically. "It is God's will of a certainty, caballeros."

An angular, very dark ranchero who lounged lazily against a far wall, spoke quietly. "Francisco—there is this imminent war between the United States and Mexico. This may solve our problem. Mexico will send troops to drive out this ragged invader."

"Invader!" Gardia spat out in vast scorn. "These are half starved outlaw wolves, nothing more. Bandits and killers and thieves—not invaders. They do not approach the name, for the love of God!" The fire subsided a little. "But no, amigos, I do not believe that. In the past Mexico has become convulsed internally, and each time she has thrown us upon our own devices. Should the United States and Mexico go to war, Señors, it will be as before. We will have our own battles to fight."

"Well then," another rancher asked plaintively, "what would you suggest, Francisco?"

26

"This—amigos. We will organize and be ready. We will send word to Pico that we *are* ready, for, mark me, gentlemen, when the time comes to fight, it is he who is prepared and ready who will win!"

A long silence filled the room. The men were comfortably exhausted from dancing and their bellies were complacent and rumbling discreetly with much good food. Juan looked around and thought to himself, wryly, that probably the best time to arouse Californios, is when they are a little lean from hunger and a little irritated with some discomfort. His head came up when Francisco began talking again.

"With your sanction, then, caballeros, I'll take it upon myself to organize us, and each of you will help. Every horseman with a lance, a gun, a lariat and a good caballo should join us. Gentes de razon, vaqueros—all; just leave your Indians at home and untrained for war. God knows they are poor fighters—only excellent thieves." This drew a chuckle and the meeting broke up shortly afterward. Juan went back out into the noise and vivid scene of the fiesta, and saw Carmen standing by herself, watching him come across the room. Instantly, his mask slid into place as though nothing had occurred between them. That she was only Augustin's granddaughter. He bowed, avoiding her eyes at first, then looking boldly for anything that might betray her thoughts.

"Juan—I'm miserable."

He said nothing, watching her, seeing the agony in her eyes and cursing himself uncomfortably.

"It is like a poniard in my intestines, Juan. It is a shame unbearable."

Wonder began to sway him a little. "What is it, little Carmen?"

She seemed to grow taller, slightly, and formidable

27

looking, then the defiance failed her. "Juan—Elena took Hernando riding with her!"

The jolt almost made him stagger. It was more than a surprise, it was also an awful suspicion. A dawning knowledge of the savageness, the primitiveness, of Elena Gardia. It wasn't Hernando Vaz she was striking at—no. It was the same inherent cruelty that had motivated Torquemada. The same incredible finesse that had scourged the soul of Pizzaro when he killed the thousands in Peru. It was, in short, the ultimate in Spanish vengeance. Strike down not only the hated, but make his own suffering greater by the agony of close friends. Juan swore viciously in English. Carmen, not understanding, comprehended nevertheless.

"Where did they go, Carmen?"

The black eyes were sardonic when she answered. "To your oak knoll. It was not her secret, Juan. She didn't want it to be. Holy Mother! It's not that she wants Hernan'. She'll ruin him though, Juan; make a madman out of him as she has others before him. I know this, if you don't. All the women know this. She is so inconceivably evil; so devilish, Juan." Carmen's chest was rising and falling with a passion barely under control. Her pretty face was as pale as dirty snow. "Then I'll get him back, when she's through with him, but not the same Hernando Vaz. Never again the same vaquero. And I'm supposed to take the ravelings of his body and try to nurse a soul back into it. All this—Juan—when everyone will know what I must do. Take this imbecile who has been like a son to my grandfather, and keep the secret of his shame, and try to make over what this—witch—has cast aside." She jerked her head a little. "And Francisco Gardia—what of him? And my grandfather, who has raised

28

Hernando—I must be the bulwark there, as well."

Juan bowed stiffly when the storm had spent itself. The grayness of his eyes was darker by shades. "Excuse me, Carmen."

She reached out a hand for his arm but he avoided her. "Juan—you don't even carry a knife."

He shook his head. "No, this isn't a situation for a knife. This may be a battle, not of steel."

Carmen looked her absolute disbelief. "You're wrong. You do not understand. She turns them into devils. You think its a manner of speech, but it isn't, Juan. It will not be the old Hernan' at all, but a flesh and blood devil."

Juan nodded without speaking, half hearing, and went past her towards the great doors and the early night beyond where the blackness was down in full glory, its majestic, velvety softness unfurled like an endless mantle that covered the entire universe with coolness—and sorrow.

Juan got a horse from the remuda near the Indians' huts, swung up after fastening his great spurs, and rode at a Spanish walk—a sort of jog—out on the dusty, parched yard, heading upland into the gloom that spread everywhere, relieved only by the weakest, wateriest, of moons.

His feelings were in a turmoil that calmed themselves gradually, banking the coals of almost inarticulate fury against a glowing hatred of Elena Gardia, as he rode. No man can stay completely angry for two hours a-horseback, and Juan was no exception.

"Mira, vaquero!"

Juan heard the words long before he saw the forms, then they materialized, wraithlike, in the heavy shadows that slunk around the gaunt skeleton of his house. He knew, before he reined up and looked down at them, that the soft music of his rein chains had warned them amply.

They were standing near the completed shop building, looking up at him. Hernando's face was slowly relaxing as recognition came to him. He was guilty looking, but still, the boyishness and good cheer were not far beneath his discomfort at being caught there, with Elena Gardia.

"Chihuahua, amigo!" Hernando said. "It is as I told you." He was nodding uncertainly up at the silent, erect figure on the horse. "The dampest of graves, indeed!"

"Hernan', do you also recall what I said about that sea of sorrow?"

"But of course, amigo. Still—there is this other thing as well. Ah," Hernando turned to Elena, who was standing perfectly still, looking up at the handsome, unsmiling silhouette against the dark sky, "he is an old one, Señora. So old in so many things. So solemn," he shrugged, "and thoughtful."

If Elena was going to speak, she didn't get the chance. Juan's anger came back. "Hernan', how big a fool is it possible for one man to be? Know you that her husband—that bull—is at the fiesta, also? Know you—fool—that he can break you with his hands. Go back instantly, for if you've forgotten the Perez's— imbecile—remember Francisco Gardia!"

Hernando threw back his head in the reckless, proud way he had, and laughed. "Amigo! I am no novice at that sport."

"And what of old Augustin?"

Hernando sobered slightly, but the wild, hot light was still in his eyes. "That—vaquero—is my affair. Have you said enough, then?"

Juan looked past the hardening face of his friend to Elena. He was beginning to feel an uncomfortable awe for her. Carmen's warning came back to him. 'She turns them into devils'.

Naturally, Juan didn't believe any such thing possible. Shifting his weight a little on the horse's back, he saw her match stare for stare with him, and wondered if there wasn't really, after all, some adroit league possible, in some way, for such things to be. Surely, there had to be a source—an origin—for this satanic behavior in a human being. They weren't born with it. It had to come into them from somewhere. Elena smiled a little, perhaps reading his bewilderment and uneasiness.

"What kept you, Juan Martin?"

He didn't answer, shifting his glance to Hernando and seeing that vaquero's growing impatience.

"I want to talk to you." She reached out and touched the brawny shoulders in front of her. Hernando turned a little, his feelings for her as plain as daylight in his face. "Go back, Hernan'."

He leaned toward her slightly from the waist. "You are trading me for this hombre, then, Señora?" The words were like silk.

"Don't be a fool. I'll send for you. It won't be long, my Hernan'."

Hernando's fingers were toying unconsciously with the dagger in his sash. He was trying to read her impassive face, but saw nothing there, and felt his own satiated dullness with some complacency.

Juan watched them aghast. Hernando's face told the story as plainly as words would have done. The tableau appalled and sickened him. Carmen had been so pathetically right. They would each, in their way, fight him. He felt confident to take care of Hernando's poniard, but the wiles of Elena—he didn't know.

Hernando went around the side of the house, caught up his horse, leaped into the saddle and rode down the night without a backward glance, his good natured features ugly in a sordid, grotesque mask that approximated madness, to a degree.

Juan unhorsed, looped the plaited reins by the romal in a low limb of a young oak and went over by Elena. His eyes were cold and unpleasant when he stopped, facing her.

"Did you do this because of me, Señora?"

"I did. Need you ask, Juan Martin?"

"If you hate me—as you must—need you stoop to such a thing as killing a man's soul?" He was still thinking of Carmen's words. "And risk the great pain this will give Carmen and Augustin Perez as well as your husband; all for your revenge?"

Elena shook her head slightly. There was no smile on the fullness of her mouth or in the opaque black eyes that looked into his face. "Juan, I'm not contrite. It brought you to me."

The anger was dammed up behind his teeth. "There is no way to undo what you have done. You are aware of this?"

She shrugged slightly. "No one will know."

"Hernando will," he shot back at her. "You used him as bait, Señora. Do you think he'll forget it like you have?" He shook his head. "He'll be at your feet from now on!"

"Holy Mother, Don Juan Martin, you are what I thought you might be, then."

It was an enigmatic, irrelevant thing to say. He was jarred away from his fury by it, puzzled "What are you talking about?"

32

"You are untamed, then, beneath this aloofness. This little smile and the gravity of the gray eyes. You are a man of passion, as I gambled you were."

She took three small steps and was close enough for the cloth of her bodice to rise and fall against the cloth of his short coat. "I told you once, being married to a man so old is only a goad to a woman."

"Then why did you marry Francisco in the first place?"

"Because he fascinated me. Like a bear, with his hugeness, his great muscles and fullness." She made a face. "And I found him a shell. Oh—there had been a beast there, once; who can doubt it? But *I* didn't get it; it was gone—the depthless passion and virility, and I married the empty covering.

"Look you, Juan. What must it be to a passionate woman, to be married to one whose friends are also old and worn out? What is it, can you imagine, to play a part forever, that you detest? Then—when you find something you need, have it snatched away and cut down by this great, hollow shell, because of his wild jealousy. Yet he, himself, may God strike him dead, can do nothing about the agony I live with. What must this be, can you imagine?"

He was shaken by the intense bitterness in her face and said nothing. Her hands went out and upwards, slowly, grasping his shoulders to her, held in a state of near hypnosis while the black eyes widened and laid a soul before him.

"Juan—can you find it in your heart to hate me, then? Have I caused more than passing pain to your friends and your Hernando?"

The fingers were encompassing more of him, pulling him toward her, but he didn't move and she was projected up against him, and he felt the fragrance of ragged breath ricochet off his upper lip when her mouth sought his.

He jerked back once. A short, savage step, then his hand flashed dully, opened and extended, and the jolt of the blow sent her sideways, horror stricken, moisture jarring out of the corners of her eyes. She fell heavily to the ground and didn't move, but lay there looking up at him in the wildest, most unbelieving shock.

The night was a great, pregnant giant of some kind without shape or features; just pustules of sickly white that were the stars. It had become as evil and unclean as it had been beautiful before. He looked down at her with a scornful twist to his face, making each feature ugly in the extreme.

"Scum! May the God in Heaven strike you down dead and your soul be the name of every dog of a dog that sees it!"

Elena came out of her shock with a wild tossing of skirts, then she threw herself at him. There was the silvery, ghostly shine of watery moonlight on the stiletto in her hand, but Juan had seen it and was prepared, moving forward on light toes that dragged the great spurs through the dust. He caught the descending wrist and twisted until the knife fell, then Elena was in against him again, sobbing and twisting, writhing with the strength of ten men and the fury of a demon, until, inexplicably. Juan knew, even before it happened that the wildness in his own blood was responding.

He fought against it physically and mentally, trying to throw her off, cursing and reviling her in Spanish and English; becoming more incoherent in his frenzy. A devil, of a certainty, going out of her and into him, and his great, good battle was nearly lost before he tore

34

away.

The night shuddered inward upon itself fitfully when a little breeze stirred the oak leaves above them, and they stood apart staring at one another, exhausted. Worn and spent and weak.

Juan stared at the blackness above. At the little stars and the huge emptiness between each one that was Eternity, and groaned aloud, once, then bit back the rest of his anguish.

There was a very real fear within him now of her. Fear and a sense of physical trembling. He heard the rustle of her skirts beside him but didn't look at her. She was staring across at him like a dark angel, fallen. She felt some of the aura of fear that emanated from him and stole away to her horse, mounted and rode back toward the fiesta again, slack-mouthed and overcome, with a fierce intentness that robbed her absolutely of every vestige of strength.

Juan turned when she was gone and stared down the slumbering land after her. The gray eyes came back to normal gradually, much later, but there was a new, awakened fearfulness in them. A savage, irrational awareness of something else within the body, besides what had been there before. A flake of brimstone, perhaps, or a coal of Hell's fire—but something, anyway, that had come out of Elena Gardia and entered Juan Martin.

CHAPTER 3

THE MATANZA WAS STARTED BY A JUEZ DEL CAMPO who came and rode through the great herds of wicked-eyed long-legged cattle with their murderous horns,

35

searching out foreign brands. This of course had earlier been taken care of by Rancho Dan Diego Del Carmelo riders. There was only the spidery, artistic brand of Augustin Perez on the animals gathered at the matanza grounds—the slaughtering area of the rancho.

Sweat dripped copiously from every face, for the sun was a huge, sweltering blister in the faded sky. Juan and Hernando escorted the Juez Del Campo away from the matanza area and returned side by side. Each in his own way antagonistic, and neither comfortable because of this sensation, either.

Juan looked furtively and saw that Hernando's boyishness was still there, but something else was there as well. A harshness just beneath the surface. Juan noticed it without being the least conscious that in his own face and gray eyes there was the identical acid of spirit.

They were close to the herd in their silence, then Hernando spoke, not looking at Juan, but instead staring his concentration at the milling cattle held in close confinement by the neophytes—the ex-Mission vaqueros; the "gentiles" as many still called them.

"Juan—as a friend I warn you!"

He said no more nor looked over. Juan was startled. He glanced across, saw the cold, uncompromising profile and followed the black eyes out over the herds and Indians, who were watching them both, waiting for the signal to begin the slaughter, and later, the nuqueo.

"Hernando, I care nothing for your warning."

The swarthy face swung around in ferocious anger. "As God is my witness, Juan Martin, if you go near her I'll kill you!"

"I?" Juan said evenly. "I was wrong, of course, in what I did. Even so, I risked nothing more than the

Gardia's happiness and my own. This is no excuse, I know, but you, Hernan'—you are risking much more. You think I don't know you've seen her since the fiesta? I do, though. And what of Carmen and Augustin, as well as the Gardias' and yourself?"

"Madre de Dios! You are imbued with the thought you are my confessor, then? What is my affair, I keep as mine!"

Juan leaned forward in the saddle a little. His anger was thick and lumpy in his chest. "I tell you this, Hernando Vaz—and hear me, for I mean it! If you break Carmen's heart and disgrace Augustin, I'll skewer you to the wall and leave you there to hack your way back to Elena Gardia!"

Hernando nodded formally, very coldly. "We understand one another, then."

"No!" Juan said with a violent shake of his head. "I don't understand you at all, and never will—until you see this madness. Hear me, imbecile. What will you get out of it but a dishonest conquest? Nothing! Less than nothing, for if I don't kill you—and you have my word that I will—there is still Francisco. Is it, then, so good to contemplate lying in 'the dampest of graves,' knowing what those who pass above, spit on your mound?" Juan let his sudden fury subside. "Hernan'—for the love of God—think!"

"And you," Hernando said harshly, "having seen her—been with her—you have turned away?" Hernando gave his head a brusque, angry shake and the poblano with its low crown and stiff, flat brim, wagged vigorously. "Remember you, Juan Martin, I'm not married, even as you're not. The choice lies with me!"

"Of course it does," Juan said dryly. "And perhaps you have devised a way to marry a married woman!" He felt the fury coming back and made a quick, savage motion with his hand. "Enough of this. You are beyond reason."

Hernando's eyes were filling again with a tawny ire when he saw old Augustin riding up oh his mule. He said no more, only jerked his head so that Juan would know.

"Mira, vaqueros!" The old voice sang out in scratchy tones of age, "Vaminos! Let us begin. The slaughtering schedule is late already. The brig will be here before long and I have this debt to pay, plus new purchases to make."

Juan sat where he was, but Hernando rode abruptly down toward the matanza grounds, seeing the two rows of riders, one in close to the herd holding it, while the others, farther out, were exclusively for cutting back bolters, which there would be after the smell of blood and offal filled the air.

Juan looked over toward the little group of Indians around the immense iron vats where the peladores—strippers—were lounging, honing their knives and loafing. He didn't want Augustin to see what he knew was still on his face. Bitterness and anger.

"Juan—You aren't going to rope with Hernan'?" Augustin's voice indicated his astonishment. Juan Martin and Hernando Vaz had roped together nearly three years. It was almost a tradition at the matanzas. Juan the heeler, Hernando the front-end man.

"Not this year. We may next season." It was very lame but on the spur of the moment nothing better would crystallize in his mind.

"Ah," Augustin said, keeping his eyes narrowed against the brilliant sunlight, and on Juan's face. "Tell me something, amigo. Hernando and Carmen are like

38

sister and brother. Is this not so?"

"Of course," Juan said, puzzled, "it is well known."

"And you," Augustin said, still staring, "you are in love with Carmen. Is this not a fact less well known? Isn't it possible, then, that you and Hernan' have quarreled over her?"

The air went out of Juan's lungs with a rush. Augustin waited like a wizened hawk, reading the incredible amazement, and let his eyes drop away and go to the herd below.

"I knew it was something. I saw this change in Carmen." He didn't raise his eyes. "What must one do?" He raised his face finally, looking at Juan. "I only live until she is married—you both must know this. How can such a choice be made?"

Juan's throat was constricted. Old Augustin with his simplicity, his tremendous innocence! He turned away, lifting the reins in his hand and hearing himself speak in a voice that was strange.

"Señor—it is getting late and the cattle are restless. Shall we commence?"

"Si, Juan, of course."

Juan rode slowly toward the herd and held his arm aloft. Instantly the pairs of riders began circulating through the herds, riding slowly, languorously almost, easing and cutting out a victim, pushing him—or her— toward the outside of the gather, then, with their animal separated, snaking riatas that never missed—rawhide that came alive in their owner's hands—through the still, heavy air and catching the luckless critter by the hind legs from one end, neck or horns by the other.

The peladores waited until the savagely battling animal was stretched helpless, then one went forward and, with a practiced, sure plunge, drove his dagger just

39

behind the poll, separating the vertebra, and the death struggles began. Almost as quickly, the rest of the strippers fell upon the animal and began fleshing away the hide.

The process was repeated endlessly and Juan's rope, with its protective coating of thin mutton tallow, got slippery in his hand. He had an Indian vaquero as his partner—a grizzled, silent man, nearly as certain with his riata as the Californios themselves.

Several times Hernando and Juan came up to the peladores with their struggling victims at the same time. It was as though there was a vacuum around them. The Indians looked significantly at one another and said nothing. The gente de razon vaqueros, Mexican, possibly, or half-bloods with a little of Castile to straighten their backs—and vast prides—noticed too. A pall of wonder fell over the mantanza, and then, with the near setting of the late sun, old Augustin rode down from his shady knoll and beckoned both Hernando and Juan to him.

"Hombres! It grows late. By my tally we are still some fifteen hides short. Shall we commence the nuqueo, then?" Both men nodded, saying nothing. Augustin's eyes swept over their set, rigid faces with a sadness that cut Juan hard, under the heart. "Then as you wish caballeros," the old man said, and turned away without another glance, reining his mule back up the slight incline toward his observation post.

Juan saw the slumped, wizened shoulders and let his gaze drop to the ground. "Hernando—you have already picked your nuqueodores, no doubt?"

"No doubt."

"Bueno. Do you wish to kill the eight or the seven? Augustin says we are fifteen short."

"I leave this to you. It is of small importance."

Juan winced at the tone. "I'll take the eight, then. Adios and—good luck."

"Adios," Hernando said, adding nothing more. He spun his fresh horse and rode back the way he had come.

On an instinct Juan glanced up the hill. Augustin was sitting perfectly still, leaning forward a little, looking down at them. The old man's pathos was clear in every line off his body. Juan spun his mount and rode back, stripping off his short jacket as he went, and reaching down for the poniard, razor sharp, he now wore Californio style, in the garter just below the knee.

Because Juan's peinado was not in the Californio style—he didn't like the feel of long, bushy hair—he had no need for the bandanna a vaquero held out to him and shook his head, as he handed over his jacket and poblano.

The old Indian who had roped with him, rode up with a self-conscious little smile. "Señor, I have a message for you."

"Si?" Juan was puzzled and saw that the Indian was vastly embarrassed and squirmed in his silla-vaquera. "It is from the Señor Gardia. He sent an Indian from the Rancho San Buenaventura, Señor. You are asked to come there this evening, after the nuqueo."

Juan's mind went instantly to Elena. A ruse, assuredly. His coloring deepened under the perfectly blank look the old vaquero was giving him. His heart was sinking, too. He could tell from the Indian's look, it was common gossip then, that he had been with Elena Gardia. If they were saying these things of him—who had only seen her once, what, then, were they saying of Hernando, who was her slave in all things, now? And—

41

more important—how long would it be before old Augustin would overhear the servants in his house speaking, and know then what shame was threatening his house, and what was making little Carmen eat her heart out!

"Señor . . ."

Juan flushed. "Pardon me, vaquero. Thank you."

The Indian turned his horse gravely and rode away, puzzled by the sudden absence of mind that had made the caballero forget him entirely.

Juan rode toward his selected riders indifferently, looking at them. Those with modish hair-dos were wearing the bandannas; those with the currently popular shorter styles of hair were sitting their horses, as Juan himself was, in shirt sleeves, with their daggers held in the right hand.

"Vaqueros, each of you take one animal. I will take two. We need only eight. Señor Vaz will take the rest Are you ready, amigos?" The curt nods were almost in unison. Juan turned, waved a hand to Augustin and stole a glance at Hernando's men. They had already signaled. Augustin looked gnomish in the distance, then his old fashioned espada—sword—raised in the fading light, poised for a second and descended like a living shaft of silver.

Immediately the closer riders spread out a little, giving the herds more room to expand and maneuver, while Juan and his chosen riders rode away from one another, watching the milling, alerted cattle, fanning out farther and farther, waiting for an animal to break and run for it.

It was the wild yell of Hernando Vaz running after a madly fleeing Spanish cow that made Juan's herd go to pieces. There was every element of savagery in

Hernando's scream. Almost as one the herd broke loose and dodged among the herders. Immediately, the dust arose in a blinding cloud scented with the sweat of animals, and Juan picked his first victim, rode in close—so close that his outstretched arm hung for a second over the fiercely bobbing head with its vicious horns and great, lolling tongue, then the arm descended like a piston, rigid and forcibly, driving the poniard into the skull behind the poll, severing the spinal column where it enters the head.

He almost followed the animal to the ground, so suddenly did it fall. His horse, wise in the ways of the nuqueando, side-stepped and lunged in a wild leap to avoid the sprawling, churning carcass. Juan's hand held a generous portion of the mane as well as the reins. That alone kept him astride. He was breathing air into his lungs that felt like hot tar when the horse caught his lead again and went on, waiting for the smallest pressure on the reins to bring him alongside the next victim.

Someone cried out in a high, wavering voice and Juan turned in time to see man and horse go down in a flurry of hide and horns. He was reining up when two herders raced in for the fallen man, then he turned back, saw a huge black bull nearby and rode after him.

The sun was red and sullen, sliding down behind distant jagged peaks, when Juan came up alongside the beast, poised his knife, eased the horse out a little more, and struck. The bull let out a roar of rage and tried to turn, head down, to gore the horse. Juan was forced to relinquish his hold on the knife and watched in fascination as he reined up and dodged the maddened charge with no effort. The animal's eyes were bloody when he stopped, shuddered, lowered his head—and collapsed.

43

Without leaving the saddle, Juan rode in behind the brute, heeled over and tugged the dagger loose, straightened up and walked his horse back slowly toward the oily smoke of the tallow vats, to retrieve his jacket and poblano.

Augustin came down off the hill slowly, his hat low over his face and a string of rawhide knots in one hand. He reined over to Juan, who among them could cipher and read, offering up the string.

Juan glanced at the carefully spaced little knots and nodded. "It is correct, Señor."

Augustin nodded his thanks, then glanced back intently at the slaughter scene behind them, saw his mayordomo watching the scattered bands of strippers at work, and turned back with a sigh.

"Then let us go."

Hernando caught up with them as they rode, shrugging into his jacket. The three men rode in uncomfortable silence until they entered the rancho yard where Indians took their horses, then Juan walked a little aside with Augustin, and spoke.

"Señor—if you will excuse me, I have been summoned to Rancho San Buenaventura by Señor Gardia."

"Ah?" Augustin said guilelessly. "This must mean his organizing is moving ahead then, amigo." He frowned slightly, looking past Juan to where Hernando was walking toward the big house "Strange, Francisco doesn't ask for Hernan' also, is it not?"

Juan had a misgiving then. Perhaps Gardia had heard of Hernando's excursions to San Buenaventura on his frequent recruiting trips. He shifted his weight a little, feeling in his heart he was deluding himself. This summons wasn't from Francisco Gardia, and he knew it.

44

If anyone was trespassing, this night, it wasn't Hernando Vaz.

"Quien sabe, Señor?" he said bluntly. "It may be a slight oversight—possibly."

"Perhaps," Augustin conceded. "Still, there is no better caquero in all Alta California. Well—be that as it may, I'll explain your absence. Adios."

"Adios."

Juan cleansed himself, changed his dress, went out into the warm dusk via the kitchen where he took up a slab of roast beef, saddled a fresh horse and rode in a Spanish jog for the first two miles, after the custom of all Californios who, from choice, knew only these two gaits in a horse, then eased his animal out into a comfortable gallop that kicked the distance rearward.

Rancho San Buenaventura's lights were little spillways of orange that tumbled down the whitewashed walls of the old house, ran out across the dark land and pooled themselves like golden water at the limits of their power.

Juan's horse was taken silently by a scarecrow of an ancient Indian who loitered, obviously, for just this purpose. Strangely, there were only the usual rancho horses at the rack, too. Juan's suspicions had crystallized into a certain knowledge that, not only didn't Francisco Gardia send him that summons, but also, the master of San Buenaventura was not at home. He stood in the warm night looking up at the house. It was folly to go in there.

He felt a premonition and looked aloft, a little, at the high sky. There was a beautiful and passionate woman beyond the age darkened oaken doors of the house. She belonged to another man. She was faithless, cruel and capable of anything—and at his feet. A wisp of the range fragrance

45

came to him. He thought of Carmen Perez. To think of Carmen was also to think of old Augustin, to whom he owed such a debt, not of gold but of honor. He remembered Augustin's words and shook his head slowly. In his sturdy innocence, Augustin had yawed widely from the truth. He thought both Hernando and Juan were in love with Carmen. It was a monstrous thing in Juan's mind, that this other shame, as Hernando had said, 'this attraction of evil,' hung over the old head, unsuspected.

He regarded the house for a long time, then went toward it. Elena herself admitted him. It took only a glance to see that she had spent hours making herself irresistible. It made the breath catch in his throat. One glance beyond the lovely woman showed that the house was empty. It had that feel to it. She smiled, of course, but a bold look on her face made the smile unpleasant.

"I am here, Señora."

She reached for his arm, pulled him gently inside and closed the door. "I see, Juan Martin."

"We are alone—of course?"

"Of course."

"Señor Gardia . . .?"

"Away. Far away." She let him see the pensive look in her eyes for a second. "Francisco is a changed man since this trouble. I—but of course that's impossible. He's too old."

"You thought, conceivably, he might be regaining some of that passion you complained was gone from him?"

She nodded, looking up into his face. "But, we know this cannot be—don't we, my Juan? A little hard riding, a mission, that's all there is to it. Still, he is fired. But—querido—it isn't the right fire."

He was watching the rawness of her emotions kindling

in the shadowy places of the dark eyes. "Señora—"

"Elena."

Juan nodded. "Elena, I came knowing Francisco was away." He saw instantly it was worded poorly. Her lips were parted in eagerness and he rushed on. "But for a different reason than you think." The flames wavered, grew smaller and waited. "I wish an agreement with you."

"Seguro, name it, my Juan. Still—you must know what I possess is yours." She went toward him, reaching for him. He had a vivid recollection of the last time she had touched him like this. But he didn't move away.

"This, then, Señora. That you discourage Hernando Vaz. That you give me your word never to see him again, or allow him at San Buenaventura."

She didn't stop until they were close enough to touch, then she looked up into his face. "But—why should I? He served me well; brought me what I used him to bait, Juan Martin. I need him no more. Besides, he is a boy. I am not a girl to be bruised and talked to. Holy Mary! I am a woman to be loved!" Her voice grew rich and heavy with feeling along toward the end.

Juan didn't bend to the mouth that taunted him. "Your word, Elena Gardia. You'll never see Hernando Vaz again—ever!"

Elena stepped back suddenly, staring at him. "This—this is a business deal to you? A—trade?"

Juan saw the amazement and recognized the rare beauty of her, the way she had looked before this obsession had taken possession of her. He nodded. "Si, Señora, if you wish to use those terms."

"It—springs from no jealousy, then? No love of me? Nothing—more than this trade?"

The amazement was gone. In its place was an

47

incredible, uncertain something that might have been half disbelief, half fury.

Juan reached for her, pulled her in against him and held her there "Interpret it as you will, Elena. Just give me your word."

The touch of his hands made her thrill anew, but still the wound was close to her pride and she didn't forget it. Without moving, content to feel the warmth of him, she looked up into his eyes again.

"You—are trading your—love—for Hernando Vaz!"

The iron in Juan made him laugh softly, ironically, without humor showing. "Call it as you will. My end of the bargain is proven. I seek only the answer. Yes or no."

She smiled to match his mirthlessness. "And if I say no?"

He released her as suddenly as he had reached out. They stood like that, toe to toe, almost, for a long moment. Neither spoke. Juan didn't have to. The action was more eloquent than a book.

Elena's color drained slowly. "San Iago!" It was a stricken sound deep in her throat. The spell lasted only a second, then she raised one hand balled into a fist and struck him a rocking blow in the chest. There was no pain to it for all the impact. He remained unmoving. Slowly Elena Gardia took a backward step, then another.

"Juan—God in Heaven! Juan!"

If he could have felt pity for her, he would have then. She was an altogether different Elena Gardia. Not spurned, but offered what she had been born to have, conditionally. Obviously, such a thing had never occurred to her before.

It took a moment for the shock to wear away, then she

48

spoke with a low, bitter laugh, first. "You are being noble. It usually is reversed, vaquero. The woman, ordinarily, makes this offer. Juan Martin, I know you to be a great animal. As you said, it is proven to me, but why in a name, I ask you, does it come to me this way? Without love?" Her mouth quivered. "I am beautiful, am I not?" He didn't answer. "Then why, I ask you—why?"

Juan watched her and thought of the fates that create people thus. Make them dazzling, then rob them of beauty of soul—and yet leave the knowledge of such beauty, the hungers and desires manifold within them. Could it be, actually, that they could not possess any happiness but the illicit kind? If so, then, there must be a devil in them, and if this was so, why, again, unless it was the payment for former sins—here or somewhere else? Why?

The struggle within Elena Gardia was brief, however. For a while she said no more, looking at him with the same passion, but without the fire. Then she nodded, jerkily, with no grace.

"As God will is, Juan Martin. Listen to me. I give you my word, and I promise never to see Hernando Vaz again. But—we have lost a great deal tonight. If this is as it must be, then at least you are honest, Juan Martin. Could it make me love you more?" She shook her head. "God, no! I have this hope, though, that you will tire me. That I will sicken of your words, and yourself. This has happened before, caballero, but—." She said it desperately in a voice almost silent with anguish. "I don't believe this will happen—this time, and that too is ironic, isn't it?"

Juan turned abruptly and went over to a small table where there was a silver filigreed bottle of wine. He poured two glasses half full and held hers out. They

49

drank and he replaced the glasses before he said a word. It was difficult, then, too. There was little to say, nothing appropriate, just the sadness that filled him for her. Not pity, but sorrow, and his only spoken word was born of it.

"Elena . . ."

"Juan—Juan!"

She went into his arms and cringed there. He tilted back her head with a solid film of guilt beneath the more powerful passion that ruled him. He wasn't unaware of the sin in this act, but took his advantage for what it was, the sole pleasure a man could derive from something he hated himself for.

He kissed her. It was an exquisite experience. One made up of subtle pressure, fragrance and infinite pleasure.

Elena looked at him with a strained expression. "Juan—conceivably, the things I would give you—sacrifice for you—are endless. I don't lie when I say, it—has never been like this before. Never."

He didn't smile, nor look pleased; if anything his expression was glum and lugubrious. "Perhaps it is the love itself, not me, nor Hernando—or the others. Possibly it is all the softness and thrills and ecstasy, that you worship." He understood, then, why the cravings within her must go forever unrequited at San Buenaventura. Francisco was, above all else, a great bull. Even were he capable of loving her, still, it wouldn't be the same. It would have the overtones of harshness and refined brutality. Such was his nature. Gardia was made for more momentous things than the game of affection. His was the blood of heroes, warriors, even despots, but not lovers. If Elena had taken him for what she thought he might be; a quenchless lover, it was the most tragic mistake of her life, for what she assumed was huge virility, was, indeed, exactly that—but not the kind that revels in subtle passion. Another irony, in fact, the crowning irony.

She wagged her head at him. "No. I am no longer a girl, Juan Martin. I am a woman. The glory of love is long past. I know this if you don't. A woman wants love without the aches and anguish, believe me. That's what I want of you. You are wrong, mi alma. Elena Gardia loves a man because of the primitiveness of his passion and the gentleness of his touch; not for love's sake, Juan, but for his sake as a man. You can understand this?"

Juan shrugged. "Perhaps. But there is an abyss between us wider than the ocean, Elena. We could be lovers, of course. That requires only passion of which we both have ample, but we could never be more."

"How?"

Another shrug. "How can I explain it? I don't have the ability. Something like this though. Your love gives absolutely everything; mine doesn't. Yours is irrational, reckless, and cruel. Mine is built of many things, but cruelty isn't one of them."

"Juan—how can you say I'm cruel. It isn't so."

"Pardon me, Señora. How else can you explain what you have done to Hernando Vaz? What of the threat of shame you offered Augustin Perez? What of little Carmen, and Francisco Gardia? In the name of God, all of this was cruel. Don't say you wouldn't have shamed and hurt everyone of them either, for you would have. It's your nature, Elena. Cruelty. Listen, beautiful one— your love is immense, I agree, but it is also terribly close to a destructive hatred that is boundless. In a word, then,

51

your love is irresponsible, irrational and cruel."

"I am no match for you in words, Juan. Only in love. Kiss me, then, for I will tell you in all truth—I love you, Juan Martin, like I have never loved before. Call it what you will, I know only the feelings inside of me. They are for love of you. Nothing else matters."

"But it does, Elena. Everything else matters. I am a man and could easily love you, but to men there is another matter equally important—demanding."

"Oh?" she said, "and this is?"

"Amour."

She stiffened against him then took two small steps backward. He saw the frustration, the wrath in her exquisite black eyes, and wondered if she would strike him as she had done before.

"And I," she said in a strained voice, "I must live in denial?"

He shrugged. "Do you imagine your mistakes—your unhappiness should be used to bring unhappiness to the innocent?"

She didn't answer; just stared at him, motionless and beautiful. The night was warm and heavy. They stood in silence listening to the faint, far distant cry of coyotes and the myriad sound of small things going their nocturnal way. Juan felt the old sadness come back. There had to be something to say. But what? The silence grew and grew. He could think of nothing appropriate. When he spoke finally, it was awkward for both of them, because the heavy oppressive silence had changed them.

"Elena—if God could have made one of us differently—there might have been something much grander than this."

She smiled it was an expression he never quite forgot.

The look of a beautiful woman, but something else too. The look of a completely unhappy woman whose destiny had finally claimed her, crucified her and left her to dream of all that was forbidden.

"Juan—I will not give you your fool of a Hernando Vaz. If you use scorn, I will use worse scorn. Now go!"

He rode back in the tiny hours of the fleeing night with a burden of weariness, knowing her nature too well to expect a graceful surrender to the inevitable.

CHAPTER 4

WITH A NEED TO BE UNSEEN FOR A WHILE, JUAN RODE to his rancho and watched the San Diego Del Carmelo laborers at work. There was the interior finishing to be done now. Artisans among the dusky neophytes remained, working mostly in abstracted silence, molding and fashioning the inner fittings of the house.

Juan hobbled his horse and sat in the shade. His sense of failure was as consuming as he had known it would be. There was little enough room for guilt because of this other sense, until, hours later, he saw the horseman riding slowly toward him from the northwest. He studied both animal and rider for some time, trying to identify either. Gradually, with a quickening sense of surprise, he recognized Don Francisco Gardia, and his larger-than-usual mount.

The hacendado waved a massive arm at Juan and rode over. They exchanged greetings informally, Don Francisco weary and sifted over with fine trail dust. Juan, feeling every imaginable iota of uneasiness a man must feel under the circumstances.

"Juan, I am glad to see you." The big man sat down

53

on the ground as though exhaustion was a natural part of him. "I came this way in the hope that you would be here, somewhere." The man's eyes went slowly over the buildings. " 'Sta bueno, vaquero. This will be something of much pride. It is indeed solidly built." He looked up, saw the gray eyes on him and patted the ground. "Sit down, I have much to tell you."

Juan sat. "News, Señor?"

"Si. There has been fighting." He nodded at the startled look on Juan's face. "The pueblo was captured, then a Yanqui named Gillespie was put in charge. He, like all these pigs from whom you can expect nothing but a grunt, was excessively arbitrary, Señor. The people revolted and left him a choice." It was evident the ranchero relished this part of his recital. "He could evacuate the pueblo, retaining the honors of war—or fight."

"And?"

"He left."

Juan shook his head. "We have heard nothing."

"I thought not," Francisco Gardia said with a weary nod. "Then—the Californios are abroad, Juan. Partly at my instigation, partly at the instigation of Flores and Pico to the south, Castro and others to the north." The black eyes were like coals.

"Everywhere the Americans have been driven off. Still, more are coming. We know this from spies. Even a new one—a dog named Kearny—is coming over the jornada del muerto."

Juan grunted. Misgivings were assailing his mind. The first tricklings of the tidal wave were rolling in upon them.

"By the Holy Virgin," Gardia rumbled on. "We have swept this rabble from our land and they are out to sea or fleeing, Señor, licking their wounds."

"Of course, this is good."

"Seguro," Gardia went on, leaning forward a little to get more of his body into the shade. "But—now comes the crucial part. We must fight them again, finally, to keep them from returning. I must confess surprise, myself, that all this has been accomplished so easily. Still—we are the best horsemen, and every battle has, so far, been one of riders. The Americanos will learn that we are the finest horsemen in the world, Juan Martin, and have held this distinction for one-hundred years before they acquired their pitiful little independence."

"Then, what is next, Don Francisco?"

"Señor," Gardia said crisply. "There were even Yanquis on the beaches of Santa Barbara."

Juan was shaken. At Rancho San Diego Del Carmelo isolated as they were and indifferent as well, they had heard none of this.

"But they, too, are gone. Routed back to their ships. Now—the danger lies in this Kearny who rides across the desert. He must be turned back. For this reason I have ridden home." Gardia's eyes were fully on Juan's face. "After that, you can see for yourself, it will be over."

But Juan couldn't see. Instead, he felt it was the beginning. The commencement of the final tragedy. "If God is willing" was all he said.

"He will be!"

Neither man spoke for a while. The somberness of thoughts occupied them fully, then Francisco Gardia looked up again

"Don Juan, I have enlisted sixty caballeros to ride south with me. Do you recall, amigo, what you said at the fiesta not too long ago?"

Juan nodded. His blood was coursing sluggishly under this new trouble that had arisen, unbidden. "Yes. I remember it very well."

"Of course," Gardia said, relieved, "you will be the sixty-first, then. This is agreeable with you? We will leave within a few days, a week perhaps, for it will take a little time to get together what we'll need." The big man sat like a mahogany buddha, cross-legged, his thick arms lying forgotten in his lap.

"Si, Señor. I'll be ready when you send me word. A good horse, a gun, the riata and perhaps a lance?" Juan's eyes were solemn. Something had arisen to snatch him away from the troubled land of his choice and plunge him into a war against his own blood. As distasteful as it was, the paramount thing, now, was to escape from the black eyes that seemed to look through him with the glassiness of a fanatic, and likewise, with the same singleness of purpose that makes fanatics so blind.

"Possibly you are a born soldier, Juan Martin. These are exactly the articles you'll need."

Gardia arose heavily, looked uncertainly at Juan as though he had more to say, then turned, removed his horse's hobbles, slid the bit into his mouth and swung up. The look of concentration remained, however, and Juan arose, looking up at him, wondering. Finally, Gardia seemed to reconsider. He made a small, annoyed motion with one hand, half-apologetically.

"Don Juan, there is this other thing." A new timbre crept into the man's voice.

Juan nodded, noticing. "Yes?"

"Possibly I shouldn't mention it. You and I, both will be gone before long. Still—I know you will wonder why I haven't asked Hernando Vaz to go with us. It is because his sight is distasteful to me, amigo." He shifted a little, tiredly, in the saddle.

"When one has servants, Señor, there is always this gossip, as you know of course." Juan nodded silently, feeling his heart stumble within him. "Well—know you then, amigo, that, while I didn't miss my wife at the fiesta recently, others did and tongues must wag." He shrugged again, half-apologetically.

"That they linked her name with yours I am prepared to ridicule, but—there is Hernando Vaz . . ." The dark eyes were more tired than angry; more melancholy than accusing.

"I speak frankly, Señor—and I ask no accounting. Only this I have to say. For you, Don Juan, I have grown a great liking; please—don't make me lose it. For Hernando Vaz—whom I know comes often to San Buenaventura in my absence, and who is a boy in his mind—I have regret. I am asking you, as his friend and companion, to pass this on to him. The next time he visits San Buenaventura while I am away, I will kill him. God is my witness to this, Don Juan."

Juan knew he was supposed to show anger, resentment and perhaps outrage—but he didn't. This was another weight added to the burden he was already carrying. Right then, anger was not only out of his mind, but a ridiculous luxury he couldn't afford. He could have forced it, but forced anger deceives no one, least of all a man like Francisco Gardia, to whom this dubious virtue was second breath.

He did bow stiffly, though, with a cold look toward the ranchero. "I will see that Hernando Vaz receives your message, Señor; still—it seems more proper that you deliver it yourself."

"No," Gardia said quietly. "In this instance, you and I know differently. Look you, Juan Martin. Hernando Vaz is a fiery youth. Instantly, there would be trouble. You can understand, then, that I do not want to kill this imbecile—just warn him off. I am not unjust, Don Juan. I only desire him to acquire wisdom in this matter. As his friend, you could do this where I could not."

Juan wondered what Gardia would say—think—if he knew that Hernando Vaz and Juan Martin were already at daggers points over this same subject and that, surely, such a message delivered by Juan Martin, would come close to provoking the battle Francisco Gardia wished not to occur. He shrugged and nodded to the ranchero.

"I'll pass this along, Señor. That is all I can do."

Gardia nodded. "Of course. I am grateful. Adios, amigo." He reined the big horse around, touched his poblano and rode away.

Juan's mind was offered a solution to the problem of Hernando Vaz before Gardia had ridden ten feet, but there was no way, with honor, to mention it. If Hernando rode with them to the war, Elena's enslavement of him would be broken, at least to Francisco Gardia's satisfaction, anyway.

He watched the hacendado cross the range until he was small, and conflict churned within him. There was, for example, the candor and honesty of the husband, the deceit of the lovers, and the burden of guilt against those who offended a man, who in turn, offered amnesty when every tenet of his environment was violently against it.

Juan cursed, suddenly conscious that his abortive pact with Francisco's wife had been a foolish thing. He turned to his horse, mounted and rode back toward San Diego Del Carmelo. He considered riding away. It struck him as a way to elude a considerable portion of his trouble at once. He would have a legitimate, even expected and laudatory reason for leaving, with

Gardia's force. He spat on the hard earth wryly. No, there was no such thing as honor, to Elena. If he went away, she would know why. Even if he was sincere in his desire to fight the invaders, she still wouldn't believe it. There was no rationalizing to her at all. Black was black and white was white. He either stayed or left, both hinged on her. Leave Hernando alone, or not, Juan would have to stay, now, for Carmen's sake; for Augustin's sake.

He was trapped, too, because, regardless of the way Elena Gardia arrived at the conclusion that he would be running from her if he left; no matter how illogical the reasoning that led her to this idea—it would be absolutely right!

The same somber line of thought brought him to another tangent of the same situation, too. Hernando Vaz could ride to the war with them. But there would be other Hernando Vaz's after they were gone, and the same vortex of peril would be perpetuated—even heightened, possibly, because assuredly Elena's wrath would strike out at those she knew Juan Martin would leave behind; Carmen and Augustin Perez.

If there was a civilized way out, Juan concluded on the last lap of his homeward trip, he didn't know what it was.

Hernando was in the yard when Juan dismounted. Even at the distance of four hundred feet, Juan could tell by the straight back and the arch of the neck, that Vaz's spirit was raging. He turned his horse over to an Indian and walked toward the vaquero.

"Hombre, walk a little ways with me."

Hernando complied, but without speaking. They went to an ancient oak, stunted and gnarled with the patience of an eternal sufferer a land of frequent and prolonged droughts.

"I met Don Francisco at the oak knoll. He was returning home."

"You were fortunate then," Hernando said dryly, "that he didn't arrive ten hours earlier. I knew, of course, that he wasn't at San Buenaventura when Augustin told us at supper, whence you had been summoned."

"You said nothing—of course?"

"Of course."

Juan nodded without looking up. "I am to pass you this message, and I said I would—although God knows it applies to others as well as you. If you visit San Buenaventura again in his absence, Hernando, he says he will kill you."

There was a sound of expelled breath through Vaz's flat lips, held so over his teeth before he answered. "You speak well, Juan Martin. This should apply to us both." He was silent for a moment, a little of the stiffness going out of him. Juan hoped for something different from what he got, from this indication of reflection. "The devil fly away with him, then."

Juan glanced up and was startled by the fury he saw in Hernando's face. It struck him forcibly that this must have been the identical expression that graced the features of the two former lovers Francisco Gardia had killed for this same trespassing. It almost made him shudder. It was proof to his mind that an actual devil was looking out of a man's eyes, twisting the features to show his triumph; offering, maybe, the testimony of destruction to the body he now inhabited, Hernando Vaz's.

Juan was badly shaken. Perspiration leaped out between his shoulder blades. Hernando's next words

60

were heard with no sense of surprise.

"Will he—the dried out old bull? What then, does he think I'll be doing? Does he imagine a man with his shriveled guts can keep such a one as Elena? Chihuahua! And you—meddling old one, believe me, I have warned you once. There will be no second warning. Do not go near her again, upon your life!"

"Listen for a moment," Juan said, suddenly, to his great surprise very calm. "I neither want to fight you or argue with you. Your warning can't change me and you know it. I ask you, Hernando, to forget this thing. It is madness—and worse."

"And you, of course, will do likewise," Hernando said, as dryly as summer wind in corn husks. He shook his head. "Perhaps you should have begun last night, Don Juan. All right, you have my warning. God is witness to it, remember that."

Juan didn't reply. He walked away, back out into the fierce sunlight and went toward the house. He knew Hernando was motionless, watching him. This caused no discomfort or alarm, but as he approached the house he knew that the height of folly had been to plead with Elena Gardia.

She had Hernando's soul as firmly chained to her as it was possible to get it. Almost as though the links were tangible and heavy.

He was uneasy in his mind. There was for a fact, something diabolical at work here. If Elena had made the bargain with him, the damage was still done. Hernando could not be turned aside now, even by the woman who had led him along this road of destruction and shame.

"Juan. Come here a moment, if you will."

He was jarred out of the sanctum of his thoughts,

61

looked up and saw Augustin wearing a harassed look, and went inside to him, where he stood just beyond the door. "Si, Señor, what is it?"

"Mother of God! Please—these beads and knots cause a brain fever." The old hacendado rolled back his eyes in exaggerated annoyance. "Time was, vaquero, when a man had only to work at living. Now, however, he must think endlessly of bales of hides and botas of tallow."

Juan grinned, refreshed at the old man's indignation over a situation that was formidable to one used to looking over the hook of his Castilian nose to distant places where honor lay in conquest, and riches were for the stout of heart—not hunched over a table with quills and leather tallies that exasperated an impatient brain.

"Come then, Señor." Juan started toward the hallway that gave access to all but the three principal rooms, then slowed gradually, remembering what Francisco Gardia had said. The Americans had been at Santa Barbara, fighting was spreading, and the invaders had been chased back to sea. He turned, waiting for Augustin.

"Señor, first I have much to tell you. Francisco Gardia had news."

Augustin's face smoothed and became alert—almost pleased and serene—in an instant. "Juan, I must apologize." He shrugged with wonderful embarrassment. "You must check those tallies, of course but actually, Carmen has already tended this count." Juan's face blanked over warily, knowing something else had prompted the summons then. Augustin put a hand on his arm and squeezed a little. "It was, honestly, to get you inside to hear whatever news you may have acquired at San Buenaventura, that I called you." He smiled and dropped his hand. "I lean heavily on the prerogatives of the old, Juan, knowing they must be forgiven. Now tell me, hombre—was it as I thought?"

"Possibly. Señor There has been fighting. The Americans have been routed—temporarily."

Augustin's eyes shone. "Temporarily? Is that your word or Don Francisco's?"

Juan flushed his annoyance. "Gardia's." He then told all he had heard. They went into the counting room and drank wine and Augustin Perez listened in absolute silence to the very end before he spoke, a certain indication of his absorption—he was much given to impatient interruptions. Then he shook his head.

"Then we will have a war, Juan. No doubt of it." He shook his head. "It still puzzles me why Francisco asks only you and not Hernan'." He lifted a hand, made a small gesture and dropped it, looking thoughtfully at the younger man. "But surely he has his reasons. Juan—of this other thing—Carmen—I concede that it affects us. . . .It has been much in my mind lately."

Juan shrugged and sipped his wine in discomfort. "For Hernando I have no answer. Conceivably an oversight, perhaps, as you have said, other plans, later— quien sabe?" He arose and looked down at the little table with its profusion of disarray, showing the irritation that had held a recalcitrant Augustin Perez to its confinement. Augustin said nothing but marveled greatly nonetheless at the speed and assurance with which Juan checked Carmen's figures, found them correct in a space of moments, and didn't even sit down to do it.

"Don Augustin, there is another thing. All this turmoil will likely keep the Boston brigs away from Santa Barbara."

63

The old head jerked contemptuously. "Deprivation is no novelty to us, here." He smiled shrewdly. "Besides, Don Juan, I owe this American pirate far more on past purchases than he can hope to acquire on things we yet need."

Juan chuckled softly and nodded. He had no more affection for the American traders than anyone else had. "Then, Señor, with your permission, I'd like a moment with Carmen."

Augustin grew thoughtful again, letting his glance embrace the thick chest and broad shoulders, the gray eyes, haunted-looking, perhaps, but still level, and shrugged.

"As you wish, Juan. I have considered this predicament endlessly, and all roads lead to one conclusion. Carmen must make this choice. Look you; God wills that each of us must mature in our own way. You and Hernan' and my little Carmen are involved in your great difficulty and I would give blood—a limb even—if the solution could be found in my own experiences." He ran a damp hand along the side of his jacket. "But this is, of course, impossible." The voice grew dry as he concluded. "However—I tell you Juan— I prefer the problems of my own generation to those of yours." He smiled. "Our's were less involved. God be with you."

Juan went through the house without finding her. It wasn't until he stood in the curved, Moorish archway into the patio that a small, sad face with great black eyes caught him in a glance of pathos, and held him outlined in the opening of the archway.

"Juan?" she said, tentatively.

"Carmen—" he stopped there, knowing pretense was useless. "Look you, little one. There is no man or woman on earth worth the sadness in your heart."

The girl watched his face reading the appeal there, before she answered. Her voice was grave and quiet. There was no lassitude in it at all. Acceptance and a groping for understanding, but no self-pity.

"Juan—tell me something. I know what you thought that night of the fiesta when I told you she was possessed of a devil. Tell me now, then, caballero, did I not speak the truth? Was it a figure of speech as you thought, or was it a literal truth. Does she, or does she not have the devil within her?"

Juan didn't have to consider his answer. It was ready behind his lips. But a sensation swept over him that was a little like the suddenness of the revelation when he and Hernando had been talking, and he had seen the devil—truly. This thought recalled Elena Gardia's madness on the knoll and, significantly, the change he had felt in his own soul after he had slapped her, that first time. The thing that had taken him to San Buenaventura that night before hadn't been anything but this new sickness that had come out of her and gone into him. He remembered standing a long while at the tie-rack by his horse, looking into the sky, undecided whether to go into the house or not. He had gone, of course. The same evil that had become a part of him after that night on the knoll, had made him go in. Then he, too, had a devil within him. It was an alarming thought.

He returned Carmen's stare in the silence that had settled between them, then inclined his head once, slowly. "Yes, I'm sure you were right then, although, as you say, I didn't believe it was anything more than a manner of speech at the time."

"Juan," Carmen said evenly, without inflection, "tell me the truth. Hasn't Hernan' changed a lot, lately?"

65

"Have you seen him? Talked to him?"

She shook her head with a small toss of impatience. "No. But answer me. Hasn't he?"

"Yes, he has."

"And this change has been evil, has it not?"

"It seems so to me, little one."

"And—he has become a servant to her—this she-devil?"

"Carmen!"

She nodded swiftly. "That is my answer."

Juan was afraid what the next question would be and was scrambling for a way to change the subject, but his mind was in a turmoil; no appropriate thoughts would fall down into the gears of his vocal box and be ground into the logic he sought. Carmen saved him, though, by leaving a subject that was gall to her as well.

"Juan—" She sat there looking up at him for a long thoughtful moment, then arose, walked over very close to him with no shade of expression at all, and held his glance. Her face was pale.

"Juan—you are alarmed? I want to tell you this, though—just once." He waited, almost holding his breath. The atmosphere was stifling. "I love you."

That was all she said, standing before him, watching his rigid face, seeing the shock spread slowly, painfully, downward from his eyes. If time ever stood still, it must have been then, when three simple words were spoken in quiet sincerity. Juan had no thought of time—everything seemed to become fixed, lasting, eternal. Gradually, reaction began. It was a delicious outpouring of something exquisite within him. Hardly aware that He was doing it, he reached for her. She came willingly enough, and they kissed, not passionately, but reverently. It was like a sunburst inside his head. A

66

cleansing, somehow, that left him strangely tranquil in mind and body. Finally he pushed her away, but not more than inches, and smiled for the first time.

"Carmen!" He was overcome with embarrassment.

"Juan—mi alma—I have waited so terribly long. If you had just raised your hand I would have come to you. The fiesta—"

He nodded quickly, glad to be back on familiar ground. "I know. I didn't know it then, for a certainty, but I do now." He made a small gesture with one hand. "It was all the other things that happened afterward—so suddenly—I had no time to understand. Can you forgive me?"

She nodded, took his hand and led him back to a bench in the patio and sat down beside him. "You need never tell me you love me, Juan Martin. When one waits so terribly long, those hopes wither—just the hunger remains."

He looked at her small, perfect profile with its thick black lashes, the curve of a perfect throat where a pulse throbbed erratically, belying the calmness of her features.

"I love you, Carmen. God in Heaven, I must have loved you from the beginning." He stopped there, fearing to add more. An irrelevant thought struck him. Here was one solution. They were in love. Don Augustin need never know how narrowly they had come to missing this feeling. He would assume Carmen had chosen Juan, herself. It would sadden him a little, as all natural solutions always do, but it would lift a weight from his heart as well. Hernando was still the orphan he had raised and the old man's pathos would go out to him. But he was bound to find peace, if not consolation, in Carmen's choice of a mate. Then the suddenness of

67

this new relationship struck him. He looked at Carmen again, fearfully.

"Can such a thing last, querida? It has been so sudden, this revelation of love."

"A Perez woman, Don Juan," she said with an archness he had never seen in her before, "is no different from any other woman in love. Conceivably, she has more pride—certainly more passion," her hand flicked quickly, sideways, to emphasize the point, "because of the blood and the vast restraint than can be released; but she can distinguish readily enough—if you cannot—the love of her soul. Does that answer you, Juan Martin?"

Juan was suddenly conscious of an aching in his legs and remembered how long he had stood in the archway. His eyes didn't leave her face and noticed the slight blush that darkened the creamy skin, then he shifted his feet and the spell was broken.

He smiled reflectively at the fearful courage that had driven her to make the declaration. "Carmen Perez—I love you. Must have loved you—from the first time I saw you. I want you to know this, before I ride away, because there is a damned good chance that I'll never return."

He had spoken several words in English. Carmen's mouth quivered. Her Spanish was voluble and explosive, coming in staccato outbursts, the words running into one another, anxious to escape her lips in order for the next freshet to emerge.

"And I love you. Don Juan, mi alma—my soul—and have prayed often for your safety. Don Augustin told us last night what he thought the summons to San Buenaventura was about—" she paused when he winced then went on, but looking at him speculatively, sideways

68

a little. "And again this morning. If you must ride to war, never forget for an instant that God is watching over you. That is all I ask of Him—now."

Her tone firmed up, then. "You will not be taken from me so soon, Juan; I don't believe He will let it happen—not so soon." She felt this was so evident a truth that she dismissed the grim prospect from her mind and smiled at him. "Now—tell me of this war, anyway, if you won't kiss me—inhabited of a devil!"

"Inhabited of a devil!" He repeated, starting violently on his bench and seeing the look in her eyes. She knew! He was stricken speechless.

Carmen shrugged. "Juan, my adored, do you think you are the first to succumb to a devil? What of those vaqueros Francisco Gardia killed? I knew them both. They were bien riatas. Understand, Juan, my soul, that God has given you back to me—from her! He has forbidden your destruction, then. Do you not see why I am so confident you will return from this war?"

She paused, looked down at the hands in his lap, reached over and took one and held it.

"Juan—that you know her is my mortification as much as yours. What man's flesh can resist a twice accursed female? The bewitching face and the devil within, as well? None, I assure you. That you are returned and here beside me is enough." She shrugged, throwing the fullness of her glance at him, unashamed, proud even, and tantalizingly. "I'm glad you have suffered too, though, because this has been nearly a sickness with me—for a long while." Her face lighted again with a smile. "Tell me of this riding away, now."

He didn't speak of the coming expedition at all, however, and she didn't insist. He reached for her, held her close to him and felt the complete surrender, and

69

kissed her. Kissed her again and again until they were both breathless, then let her go.

For a long time, an hour perhaps, they sat still saying very little, just a word now and then, each relaxed and somber, letting the waves of peace wash over them from within as well as without, entirely engulfed in the bliss they had so lately discovered.

CHAPTER 5

AFTER SUPPER CARMEN AND JUAN RETURNED TO THE patio and he told her all he knew of the troubles Francisco Gardia was so engulfed in. He added his own thoughts as well—more than he had ever said before; not just the facts, but the possibilities and probable culminations, too.

She heard him out with a gravity that was enchanting to the man beside her in the late shadows of dying daylight. Leaning forward a little, twisted, her dark eyes scarcely leaving his face, her mouth parted a little in concentration. It was all he could do to keep from touching her.

When it was all over and the hour was late and each secretly feared that at any moment Augustin would come garrulously to the doorway reminding them of the impropriety of their seclusion, she dismissed all the formidable portents with a gesture of one hand, and returned to the things close to her own heart, in true womanly fashion.

"Juan—mi alma—if Don Francisco rides away, what then of Elena and Hernan'?"

He shrugged in something akin to annoyance. With lives and futures, nations and destinies in the balance,

70

what, then, of a madman and a woman of infinite evil? His own suddenly found love filled him with such abundance that he had forgotten the Gardia woman and Hernando Vaz.

"What—little angel—of them? Look you—I haven't told you that I was asked to speak to Hernando by Don Francisco, warning him away from San Buenaventura. I carried the message and was, in turn, turned away from Elena Gardia by Hernan', on pain of death. Listen, I offered to be Elena's consort, then, if she would promise to leave Hernando alone. She would not agree—. This was last night, little one; don't look so shocked. Last night was an age ago, for us."

"She agreed, Juan?"

He shook his head. "No, but I overlooked something when I made the offer. Hernando himself. She could refuse to see him, but that would not have changed the resolve he has to see her. Do you understand, amador? I have done everything I can do, hoping to avert the shame to Augustin and you, of the certain consequences of this madness. What more *can* I do?" He answered it himself, with a shrug. "Nothing. Nothing at all. Warning Hernando had the effect of pitch on a fire, you know that."

She nodded with composure. "And, one other thing, Don Juan. This fear of yours that you may not return. Is it that the war will be fierce, then, or—something else?"

He looked over at her, surprised. "What else could it be?"

She was looking at him pensively. "Juan—to know a person is not to know them. To love a man is also to know him less than a brother. Hernando is no enigma to me, I assure you. Since childhood I have known him. There have been indeed, few secrets between us for, after all, we have grown to maturity together. But you, my own, are more of a mystery than ever." She saw his wonder growing, shaping into words and waved it aside with a movement of her head. "No, Juan, listen to me. You came to us several years ago and have learned all that we know. Still, you have given nothing beyond your goodness—nothing of yourself, you understand—and therefore, I, who love you deeply and have suffered all the anguish of the damned because of it—I know you even less than Hernan' does."

He thought for a moment she was going to say, than Elena Gardia does, and was wincing before she stopped speaking, looking down at him, admiring the beauty of his rusty auburn hair and the clear grayness of his eyes in the dark russet of sunblasted skin.

"Carmen, there is little to know. With this—this—agony removed from me, it is like losing the insufferable burden of a great weight. I am light in body and spirit, happier than I ever have been before in my life. Believe me, then, Doña Carmen Martin—" he was laughing with his eyes when he said it—"there is little to know. I love you, and imbued with the longing for our lives to go as your grandfather's life has been—and I pity with all my soul, Hernando Vaz. Pity him as much as I pity that possessor of a devil, this Elena Gardia."

"Your other life—back where you came from, then, is of no importance to you—to us?"

"None whatsoever. However, someday I'll tell you of it and you can judge, if you wish, but there's little enough of interest in it, querida."

She nodded again, reaching for both his hands and tugging him off the bench. "Then sit in front of me, I'm getting a sore back from twisting sideways like this."

Juan laughed, reached out, pulled her close, kissed

her squarely on the mouth, then he released her and dropped onto the floor at her feet, his hand propped on one palm.

"Juan," she said calmly, "you will come back from this war. I know it as well as I know in my heart that I'll be here waiting for you, making myself ready for what will be ahead for us."

They talked a little longer, letting the night shadows snuggle in around them, then he reluctantly got to one knee, brushed absently at his embroidered sleeve and shoved himself erect, flexing tired muscles.

"When will you marry me, Carmen?"

"Whenever you wish, Juan. Marry you and more than that—cherish you until we die." The color came flaming back into her face again. Finally, without the incentive of anger or near-anger, speaking words that were honest and frank without supporting or sustaining side-thoughts, she was as confused and blushing as she had been originally; the same small girl again, frightened and embarrassed and awfully self-conscious.

"Buenas noches, mi paloma."

She stood up too, looking up into his face. The temptation was too great, besides, there was the expected kiss of parting. He stepped closer, letting her fit warmly, vitally into the fold of his arms, his temples echoing with the dull thunder of their uneven heartbeats, then he kissed her gently and left the patio.

For Juan, this new feeling, with its poignant longing, was a buoyancy that filled his spirit. Sitting on his bed in the semi-gloom of a nearly full moon, he thought distastefully of sleep. Like a herd bull, he thought, dull and complacent and unimaginative, falling into bovine slumber because he is possessed of no soul.

He sat in silence listening to the big house's small

noises. Somewhere, far off, a coyote tongued toward the sky. Instantly he was answered, then a chorus of the little voices clamored, rising, falling, rising again into a crescendo of discord, then breaking off into little, individual coughing barks, here and there. He listened, understanding. They were converging on the matanza grounds where the rich, red meat was left to rot after the men had taken what they needed. There was no way to save it. Meat spoils fast in a hot country during summer; furthermore, the Californio trade was in hides and tallow, not fresh beef.

His restlessness drove him through the house to the patio again. There was a magic to the night, with its new fragrance and heavenly coolness. He sat for a while, thinking, then, still unsettled, he arose, vaulted the patio wall and went toward the corral of horses, the San Diego Del Carmelo remuda, selected an animal, saddled it, buckled on the huge spurs and swung up, riding north-eastward.

The night was one of those cool benedictions that caress arid lands. Clear, fragrant, with musty odors and primed with the mysterious energies of darkness that soothed and becalmed those who were out in it.

Juan rode leisurely, absorbing the majesty of the heavens and the somber darkness. At his rancho he tied the horse and wandered slowly through the buildings. There was an abundance of humbleness and gratitude in his heart. Augustin's laborers were nearly finished. The job was a masterpiece of severe, functional rancho architecture. The very severity left one with a sensation of cleanliness and peace. He could feel the rising of his battered spirit, and sat on the dried grass with his back against the massive wall, to wring every drop of this tranquillity from the atmosphere.

He was still there, half slumbering, remotely aware

that he would have problems to face with the new day, when he heard the horse coming slowly through the darkness. There was music of rein chains but Juan puckered his brow. The customary sound of the steel spurs was lacking.

The shadow grew, assumed perspective and substance and, after a while, a depth, then Juan arose, waiting. The rider came close, bent a little as though probing the gloom, saw Juan's horse, swung down gracefully and tied the horse close by and came on afoot. By then Juan knew. The desire to run was strong, but, aside from an inability to go far afoot, his attitude wasn't compatible. He leaned back against the wall, waiting. Recognition had come at last, and with it, distaste.

"Elena."

"Juan, I see you now. By all that's holy it's eerie tonight." The beautiful face with its perfect features, richly textured skin and large eyes swung away from him as she walked closer, looking askance at the pale outlines of white buildings. He followed her glance, but saw nothing beyond the simple majesty of his rancho, iridescent and clean in the soft light.

She went close to where he leaned. He could smell her fragrance and see the magnificent profile, both face and figure. His blood stirred in response.

"What are you doing here?"

She looked up with a half smile and shrugged. "I came to see you—who else?"

"How did you know I was here?"

The smile broadened. "Simple, caballero. A San Buenaventura Indian lay in the brush above San Diego Del Carmo all day, and tonight, watching for you to ride out. I hardly expected such good fortune as to have you come out in the moonlight." She laughed. The sound was rich and thrilling. "It took three Indios to accomplish it, my love, but it was done, as you can see."

"I see, all right," he said dryly. "Where is Francisco? He arrived home, I know, because I talked with him on this spot today."

"Do you care? I don't." He didn't answer. She could see his unsmiling face looking over at her. Another shrug. "He sleeps like a great bear—especially after these trips of his."

Juan said nothing for a while. He considered all the things he should have to say to her some time, and tried to select something appropriate, but fear held him back. If she knew he had asked Carmen Perez to marry him— that he had confessed his love of the other girl, or even that he was adamant in the desire to keep Hernando away from her, she would unleash all the vengeance of which she was capable. He shuddered inwardly, knowing there were no depths under heaven this woman wouldn't stoop to.

"Elena—it was folly to come here tonight. Francisco—"

"Francisco won't know I'm gone, but, even if he did, how could he find me? Track me in the dark, perhaps, or have followed me?" She shook her head watching his face. "None of these things. Is it that you fear him, too, my Juan?"

He shook his head irritably, saying nothing. Elena stood perfectly still looking up at him, breathing deeply of the night air. When she wagged her head it was with a certain negativeness to the motion.

"Have you seen Hernando, Juan querida?"

He heard the banter in her voice and turned toward her. "I talked to him early this morning." His mind revolted against what suddenly occurred to him. She

76

wouldn't leave young Hernando alone. She'd use him—ruin him too, and for no better reason than to torment Juan.

"Have you seen him, Señora?"

"Si, my lover, he is at San Buenaventura right now, tonight."

Juan straightened as though she had struck him. Fury began to flood his mind. "You did that? Knowing your husband will kill him?"

She smiled a little, teasingly, but didn't laugh. "You misunderstand, querida. It was like this. After you talked to Hernan, he rode to San Buenaventura."

"*After* I talked to him? But the fool knew Francisco was returned. I told him that; and that Don Francisco Gardia said he would kill Hernando if he ever—"

"I know," she interrupted. "But he came anyway—the imbecile. Now I am obliged to hide him in the Indian's hut until Francisco leaves again." She spread her hands. "What else could I do, after he came there? If Francisco had seen him—known he was on the rancho—he would have killed him, and after all—" she said quietly, "he has his uses, alive."

Juan almost sneered, but he didn't. The temptation was great nevertheless. "You, perhaps, could keep him for torture, Señora."

Elena's face lost its composure in the chill of his anger. "You know better, Juan Martin! He is like the others—an animal, yes, but a talkative, mealy, mushy one. There is—you know well—more to love than words; there is the abandon and pain, too. After you, what could a Hernando Vaz, or a hundred others like him, offer me?"

"Elena—you'll never be able to get rid of him. You may think so, but I know better. Look you, there is a madness in him that you, yourself, planted there. It will destroy him. I'm reconciled, but the day may come when you'll wish to God you had never toyed with him."

"Juan!" Her face was surprised. She looked startled as the real scorn in his face was borne in upon her. "You— are different, tonight."

"In many ways, Señora. Perhaps Hernando was an instrument—who can tell—but at any rate, you have proven your cruelty to me by seeing him, hiding him, and I no forger am obliged to treat with you as a result."

She frowned. "What else could I do?"

"Francisco said that he would kill Hernando Vaz if he ever went to San Buenaventura in his absence, is this not correct?"

"Si."

"But Francisco is at home now. He would welcome Hernando, if with reserve, at least not with a dagger in his hand, now, and you know it Do you think your husband a murderer, Señora, out of hand? Well, I don't. You have done a thing as foolish as Hernando's ride over there, and I believe both of you were prompted by the same blindness."

"Madre de Dios! You have the strength of a bull I know. Now I believe you have the cruelty as well. You think I would keep that—that, fool for friendship?" A shake of her head that made moonlight flash off her teeth. "No, Juan Martin. I keep him as a threat to you, and that's the only reason. He is the tool I'll use to force you to leave this accursed land with me. Or Francisco can have your boyish friend, for all I care!" She tilted back the beautiful face and let the weak light outline each feature to him, exposed and adamant now.

"Juan—my Juan. Francisco rides south within a week

78

or so. You and I will ride away together after that."

Juan looked at her scornfully. "You are mad. Listen to me, Elena." He had decidé he couldn't play this game with her any longer. It wasn't in keeping with the cleansing of heart that had occurred on the patio at San Diego Del Carmelo, while he was with Carmen Perez.

"No, I think not. There is the fact that you might ask me to leave with you . . ."

"Impossible," he said, striving to get back to where he wanted the conversation to be. "Tonight is the last time we'll meet. You have my word for it."

"And your idiotic friend, Señor? This fool you are trying to save from yourself; what of him?"

He snorted. "You, yourself, will likewise be exposed with Hernando. That's the end of it."

He knew what she would say next, before she said it, and was resigned, if not prepared to answer. His mind was racing ahead, searching for a way to forestall what was becoming more imminent with every second, and absolutely indomitable in his resolution not to concede to her again, even if it expedited the inevitable— Hernando's death and Augustin's shock, sadness and shame.

Elena's blood was aroused by the fierceness of her opposition to what he was doing. It brought up the full force of her fury, unrestrained disposition.

"Esta bein, vaquero. You wish it this way. You—who once accused me of planning to hurt others. Well—you will see that I can do it!" Her nostrils were flaring against the pressure of short gusts of breath. "You have come to see me this way; then I'll make you right! Let Francisco have Hernando, the imbecile, then."

"I have come to see something else, too, since you and I were last on this knoll. It is something of a devil

79

that shows destruction. I saw it once in Hernando's face, and now I see it in yours. This devil will destroy you through a madness."

"You are predicting?" she said savagely.

"Si, if you wish. I am predicting. This evil will destroy you, Elena. Both of you, Hernando as well as you. God knows I tried to stop it."

She didn't laugh, but she smiled. It was a ghastly grimace for such a handsome face, in the watery light. Then she nodded. "Carmen Perez—and old Augustin—can have their precious Hernan' back, then, stiff and sightless, in a carreta drawn by oxen from San Buenaventura, caballero. This is what you are trading for—now!"

Juan said nothing, just stood with his back to the cool adobe of his unfinished hacienda, sick within, considering the consummate evil of this beautiful creature beside him. There was no way to compromise, any longer, between them

She was staring at him, fixedly. "Juan—there is something else now; I can sense it." She paused, took a small step closer so that her dress brushed his hand, searching his face. "You—are in love with this Carmen Perez! Tell me—damn you—is this true?"

"Elena—there is much I could say, but none of it would affect you."

He pushed off the wall abruptly and turned away, going toward his tethered horse with large strides.

For a stunned moment she didn't move, then she went after him, running with quick, frantic steps until they were side by side, then she reached out and pulled him around. He finished untying the horse and held the hair rope in his hands.

"Juan! For the love of God—don't do this to me.

80

Look you—I offer you everything. Yours for the taking." She went closer and held both his arms. "Money too, if you wish. Don't love me, then, but let me teach you to. I swear I can do this, Juan. I'll *make* you love me!"

He jerked away without a word, stepped into the awkward, heavy oaken stirrup, and swung across the horse, reined around Elena's tied animal and swung southwest again, over the undulating range toward San Diego Del Carmelo.

His mind, as he rode indifferently along, was filled with the fragments of the peace he had ridden to the oak knoll with. They were scattered in a hundred dry, hot places inside his skull, and yet, strangely, his soul had an odd composure to it. The source of this strange serenity was obscure, but its influences were unmistakable. Even to the pity he felt for Elena Gardia as opposed to the certain dislike he had felt when they had talked, back at the rancho. And there was a resolve as well, to salvage Hernando's life, if it was at all possible to do so, before Elena Gardia unleashed the horror she had assured him she would use in retaliation.

He rode without effort or direction, letting the horse pick his way with a sure, equine instinct, for home. It wasn't until the sight of his own rancho was lost in the blackness to the rear and the nearby buildings of Rancho San Diego Del Carmelo were beginning to show whiter in the distance, that he heard a rider coming in toward him from the north. He pulled up on the reins, listening. There was the very faint sound of rein chains and this time, the accompanying soft music of spur rowels as well.

He saw an oak thicket and reined over behind it, wondering at another rider being out in the small hours of the night. He sat there, waiting, wondering where the rider was and knowing well it wasn't Elena, but, try as he might, he couldn't locate the man. Then the sound of the pleasant music of a horseman grew fainter in the darkness until it died out altogether, and Juan rode out again, eyes narrowed for what he knew he wouldn't see, shrugged and resumed his way homeward.

There was a mellowness to the deserted ranch yard of San Diego Del Carmelo, a certain, intangible melancholy and somberness, when he swung down, unsaddled, removed the spurs and turned the horse out again. There was also, less abstract and more penetrating, a slight chill threaded through the coolness that signaled the approach of dawn.

He turned toward the house, walking quietly, then, on a whim, veered off until he was close to the patio wall, vaulted it and took three wide steps before he stopped dead still, staring at the apparition looking up at him from the bench he and Carmen had occupied the afternoon and evening before.

"Carmen? Is that you, darling?"

The head nodded slightly. "Si—my soul—it is me. Have you been—out?"

It was the way she paused with a catch in her voice, before she put the last word in, that drew him across the patio and down beside her, feeling for her hands, finding them, cold, in her lap, and enfolding them within his own grip. The very solemnness of her glance was enough.

"Amour—I was restless, indeed. I tried to sleep; it wouldn't come, so I rode to my—our—rancho."

"And?"

He was moved to recall Hernando's often stated

82

comment that Carmen had a rare insight. It made him decidedly uneasy. The truth would sound worse than ever. He relaxed his hold on her hands in case she wanted to withdraw them, later.

"And—Elena Gardia rode up." He was looking for the confirmed suspicion that would show by the setting of her mouth, but it didn't show.

"Well—surely you two didn't just stand there in silence. What then?"

He told her all he could remember of the conversation. It sounded bad enough as he recalled it, but making no attempt to amplify or soften any of it, made it sound even worse, in the retelling, than it had when he had been involved in it.

"Then," Carmen said finally, "there is an end to the hope of shielding Don Augustin from this man he has raised and fostered as a son."

"No, not yet. I'm going to see Don Francisco tomorrow."

"What good will that do?" she asked, looking up at his face and noticing the deeper shadows where his beard stubble had sprouted through the night.

He shrugged. "Nothing, perhaps. Conceivably no good, little one, but at least you can appeal to Francisco Gardia, where no appeal on earth—or threat even—will sway his wife."

"But Juan, what then, of Hernan'?"

He made a face that showed his tolerance was fading rapidly, for his one time friend. "Again, darling, I have no idea. Something will come to me, though, I think." He turned to her, wishing to change the subject, because he did, in fact, have an idea of how to bring Hernando back to his senses. One that Carmen Perez would be aghast at.

"Tell me you love me again, querida, then tell me what brought you to the patio."

Carmen laughed softly, looking roguishly at him. "One answer for both questions, vaquero. I love you indeed, even though you sneak away at night and meet this Elena Gardia, and, it was this same love that brought me back to where I found it, naturally enough, when I couldn't sleep."

"Listen to me, Carmen. I did not sneak out to meet her."

"No," she said serenely, "of course you didn't, my Juan—but just how—in the hell—did she know you would be there, tonight?"

He was startled by the use of the three English words and showed it very plainly. "Well! Where did you learn those words?"

She really laughed that, time, but behind a hand. "From the sailors who man the Boston brigs. Is it so awful, Juan, my love. Your face said it was."

"It's awful, all right," he answered dryly.

Carmen shrugged. "I have been trying to remember every word of English I have heard and make sentences out of them." The twinkle was back in her eyes. "Maybe it would be better if I learned English from you, instead."

"I'll gladly teach you, mi amour. That and other things as well."

She dropped her eyes quickly. "You were going to tell me how Elena found you."

"Si. She told me at the oak knoll, that San Buenaventura Indians were detailed to watch San Diego Del Carmelo and carry the word to her as soon as I rode out." He shrugged. "It sounds weak, I concede, but it's the truth nevertheless. At any rate, I was alone at the

84

knoll when I heard a rider coming. It was Elena Gardia. You know the rest."

"You didn't touch her, Juan?"

"No. I had no desire to."

Neither of them said anything for a while. The chill crept in. Carmen snuggled closer to him and sighed, then she lifted her head a little and searched his face.

"Juan?"

"Yes, darling?"

"I have done something you may not approve of."

"Oh?" He was smiling gently at her. "What then?"

"I told Don Augustin you asked me to marry you, and that I accepted."

"Well—and what is so wrong about that?"

She smiled slyly. "If my memory doesn't fail me, it was I who, indirectly perhaps, asked *you* to marry *me*."

He shook his head in mock gravity. "I think not, querida. I distinctly recall asking *you*."

"Well, we are in accord and that matters most. Then—there was something else."

"What?"

"Grandfather immediately set about planning a great fiesta. It is to commence in three days. He—we—thought it should be this way, so that our marriage can be consummated before you ride away."

"Carmen, does he know Hernando isn't at San Diego Del Carmelo, yet?"

"Yes, of course, but he thinks he is out on the range somewhere, or visiting, perhaps. It isn't unusual for Hernan' to be gone for days at a time, you know this."

"Yes, I know" Juan's eyes were growing heavy. "We will be married at the rancho?" She nodded, watching him closely. He smiled and reached for her again. "God is bountiful, little Carmen. He is good to us. Come

85

here."

She went eagerly. The sun was peeking over the distant, sharp plane of the earth when they parted. A new day had come.

CHAPTER 6

DON FRANCISCO GARDIA WAS IN HIS OFFICE, SEATED amid the cluster of his rancho logs, tallies and accounts, when Juan went in. The big man looked up at him gravely, eyed him for a silent moment then arose, bowed and motioned toward a chair.

"Don Juan."

"Señor." Juan said, seating, himself and reaching for the glass of dark, oily wine the hacendado offered him.

"I am glad you rode over."

"Oh?" Juan said. "The plans are going forward then?"

Francisco nodded heavily. "Yes—that and other things as well." He moved on his bench, sloshed the wine in its glass, raised it to his lips and drank it off in a large swallow.

"Juan—we will ride soon. Perhaps in five days or less."

"Bueno, Don Francisco. I have brought a message for you from Don Augustin. He is having a celebration commencing the day after tomorrow. Naturally, San Buenaventura is invited."

Gardia's sober eyes were thoughtful, then he nodded again. "You will convey my thanks, of course. We will naturally be there. A fiesta celebrating our departure is correct. Old Augustin Perez would know this, of course, and plan accordingly, wouldn't he?"

Juan nodded, for some inexplicable reason not telling

86

Don Francisco that, really, the fiesta was a wedding celebration more than a gathering for the riders to the wars. He was considering how to bring this up, when Gardia spoke again, leaning back against the thick wall, lids half down over his eyes.

"Juan Martin—as I once said, I have grown a liking for you. We have some things in common, I believe. A love of our way of life, for one thing; an affection and loyalty to our friends for another."

Juan finished his wine and set the glass aside. He noticed how slippery his palms were, suddenly.

"But—there has arisen something that may, indeed, make us enemies."

"Señor?" Juan said, with misgiving.

"Hernando Vaz, Don Juan."

Juan's anger rose rapidly. Elena had already begun her no-quarter battle. He felt the drowsiness that had held him on the ride to San Buenaventura, slip away in a second while his mind leaped to meet this threat.

"What of Hernando, Señor?"

Gardia shrugged, still slouched, looking at Juan steadily. "He—the fool—is hiding on the rancho, waiting for me to ride away again. Tell me, Don Juan— did you convey him my warning?"

"Certainly. Señor. As soon as I returned from the oak knoll."

"And his reaction?"

Juan's palms were clammy as well as moist. He shrugged. "The same as your reaction would be, or mine, Señor. to any veiled challenge to fight. Hernando is a brave one. He—"

Gardia didn't move when he spoke, but an ironic, hard light showed in his eyes as he interrupted quietly. "Juan—I appreciate your shielding of this idiot—this friend of yours. Had he come openly, naturally, honor would forbid what I have in mind. But he didn't."

"You say he is hiding here, Don Francisco? Where do you have him, then?"

Gardia shook his head. "Not yet, Señor. It is but a matter of moments, however. He is being sought out by my mayordomo at this instant. That's why I'm here, in the office. This is where I wish to see him—to challenge him." He shrugged. "It is unfortunate, Juan, that you had to come at this time. Very unfortunate. I regret it."

"But Don Francisco—can't I appeal to your friendship for Don Augustin? Here, then, is an old one who has few years left to him. This shame and sadness will kill him. Surely, you must know this."

Don Francisco's eyes were still on Juan's features, unblinking and level. "I have thought of that, believe me, Señor. God is my witness. I have thought much of that." He waved one massive arm. "It isn't only Don Augustin, either, Juan Martin. It is also little Carmen, and even you, Hernando's friend, and there is the shame to my own name that such a fight will perpetuate. Saint Christopher, Juan Martin—what else can I do? There cannot be forgiveness after so blunt a warning. Also. know you, this affair of their's is well known. I am bound to kill him. Believe me, amigo, it makes me nearly ill. I am sick of these fights and these pecadillos. Sick to death of them." The grave black eyes wavered for an instant, showing infinite melancholy in their depths.

"This is my reward, possibly, for having lived as I have. Only God knows if this is so."

Juan was still slumped, feeling the unpleasantness of his palms, when the heavy, irregular tread of men loomed up beyond the door, and Hernando Vaz, disheveled, with a thin tracing of blood laced back over one cheek where it had whipped with the impetus of a blow, entered. There were three perspiring vaqueros, rumpled and breathing hard, behind Hernando, whose arms were lashed in popular Spanish handcuffs of grass rope, and pulled murderously high behind his shoulder blades.

Hernando's agony must have been considerable, but he didn't show it, only the surprise at seeing Juan there, with Don Francisco, and the livid anger of being manhandled. The black eyes raked over Juan incredulously. Juan understood, in an instant, what had happened. He writhed inwardly. Even Elena couldn't have planned it better; had Juan Martin sitting complacently, sipping wine with Don Francisco, when Hernando was betrayed to the husband. It was damning in the extreme. Juan saw the relief of it in Hernando's face.

Francisco Gardia didn't move for a long time. The San Buenaventura vaqueros were uncomfortable under the stare that was fastened on the captured lover by their massive, formidable employer. Finally, Francisco spoke.

"Chollo—do you know the Indian who hid him?"

A thick-haired, swarthy, pock-faced man nodded. He was apparently the mayordomo. "Si, Señor. It is Cabeza de Caballo."

Francisco nodded absently. "Head of the Horse, eh? Well—twenty lashes to his infidel back, then."

The mayordomo hesitated, shuffled his feet in anguish and screwed up his courage by prodigious labor. "Señor," he protested, "what could he do?"

"He could have refused, vaquero." Francisco said quietly.

"No, Señor. The Señora ordered him to hide this—

89

this—hombre. Had he refused, she would have had him lashed. There was no choice, Señor."

Gardia's eyes lingered on his mayordomo's ugly but fair features, then he shook his head at the man. "No, vaquero. I disagree. Had Cabeza refused, she would have told you to have him whipped. You take orders only from me, as you well know. It would have been a simple thing to delay the punishment until I was returned. You know this well, amigo, for you have acted similarly before. Twenty lashes, Chollo!"

"Si, Señor," the mayordomo said, turning with hot eyes and jerking his head coldly toward the door. The other riders turned quickly, eager to leave the blighted scene. Juan went over after them and closed the door, then resumed his seat avoiding Hernando's eyes.

Gardia made a motion toward the rope. "Juan, will you release him, amigo?"

Without answering, Juan drew his poniard and slashed the ropes. Hernando fought back a grimace of pain as the blood began flowing back into his cramped limbs.

"Sit down, hombre," Gardia said to Hernando. The vaquero shook his head coldly, giving them both venomous glares of defiance.

"In this company, Señor—I prefer to stand."

Gardia shrugged. "As you wish. Hombre—Juan Martin, here, passed you a message from me, about what would happen the next time you slipped to San Buenaventura, did he not?"

Hernando's face grew saturnine. He swung his glance to Juan and saw the discomfort there, in the gray eyes. "Don Francisco, I received your warning. I offer no excuse and no defense. If we must fight, then that may be as God wills it But this—this—pariah, here. This Yanqui

90

with the black heart—what of him?" Juan leaned forward on the bench, bracing against what he knew was coming A torrent of invective as only an aroused Californio can heap it.

"I have no regrets, Don Francisco, and go willingly enough to my punishment—grave, even—if it is to be this. But this hombre, I assure you, is not without the guilt of a traitor. What, then, of him?"

Hernando's flushed, dirty face was turned toward Gardia. There was a triumphant, satanic look in it.

The ranchero still didn't move. His eyes didn't even leave Hernando's face when he answered. "I am aware of what you imply Señor. Think you that my vaqueros are blind? That they don't tell their master exactly what transpires in my absence? I am amazed at the folly of any man who takes such immeasurable risks. Should you live longer, Señor Vaz, remember forever that any way of life that is built around the need of servants, is similar to living on top of the highest hill without shelter."

"Well," Hernando insisted, "what of him then?"

"That," the ranchero said quietly. "will be resolved in due time. It is none of your concern anyway." He pushed himself off the back wall with a begrudging effort, studying the powerful arms and shoulders of Hernando Vaz.

"Now, Señor, you are challenged." The thick shoulders rose and fell. "The rest remains with you. The time and place. If you wish, Juan, here, may act as your attendant. I will furnish the swords."

Hernando's eyes glazed for a moment. Juan watched him in fascination. A tumult of disconnected sentences played havoc inside his head. How this very Hernando Vaz had said that Don Francisco had killed his wife's lovers. How Elena Gardia would deliberately ruin a man, then toss his carcass aside, and the man would be willing to die afterward. It all boiled in his mind. That, and other things as well. His own deep suspicion, confirmed of late, that all of this tragedy wasn't man-made at all. It was a frightening madness that she spread from herself, contaminating the men she touched.

He felt his nerves crawling under his flesh. That Francisco Gardia knew he, Juan Martin, had also visited Elena in his absence, didn't surprise him as much as he thought it would have. As it should have, indeed. The other thoughts overwhelmed this realization.

He arose slowly and faced Don Francisco. "Señor—"

"Please, Don Juan, later."

He shook his head. "No, if you'll excuse me, Señor. Now. What Hernando says is true. I, also, have visited San Buenaventura in your absence. I am only slightly less guilty than Hernan' is. Conceivably, just as guilty, in a sense."

"How is this?"

Juan shrugged. "Because I, at least knew better. No madness gripped me, or, at least less, after a while—after an awakening, as it were—than grips him."

Don Francisco shook his head wearily. "Don Juan—you speak in parables. I don't understand, but it makes no difference. One at a time, if you please. I have not forgotten the rumors about you, believe me, but allow me this other one first." He faced Hernando again. There was almost despair in the black eyes. Just the pulse at his temple, that beat regularly, thickly, showed that his iron spirit was still inflexible, although considerably lessened in fierceness, than of years gone by.

"You have considered, vaquero?"

Hernando shrugged. "It is of small importance, Señor. Here, there, anywhere," another careless shrug. "Just make it soon."

Gardia nodded his acceptance and, possibly, understanding. "Bueno, then. Tomorrow at dawn. I will bring the weapons, and my mayordomo as attendant, and, perhaps," he faced Juan again, "Don Juan will attend you—if you wish it."

Hernando turned savage eyes on Juan, seemed about to spit on him, then appeared to reflect. There was a cold irony in his eyes when he nodded. "Good. He can see how this is done. Perhaps it will stiffen his back, Señor, for his own turn."

"As you will, Señors," Gardia said, arising. "Hombre, you will remain my guest until tomorrow at dawn, then." He was moving toward the door, a hulk of a man who had lost the spring to his step that once had set him apart from other men as thick, when Hernando held up a swollen hand.

"If you would summon guards, Señor, know then, that my word is sufficient."

For a second Don Francisco hesitated. He shot a look of inquiry at Juan, who nodded very slowly, saying nothing, then Gardia shrugged and opened the door. "Upon your honor then, Don Hernando. Here, at Rancho San Buenaventura at dawn, tomorrow morning. It is agreed?"

"Certainly, Señor."

Juan watched Hernando's erect walk as he crossed the room and went through the door. It stirred up anguish within him. He and Francisco Gardia sat for a long while in absolute silence, then the ranchero poured out two more glasses of the heavy wine and they sipped it in a macabre quiet that grew and grew until it was like a weight on Juan's shoulders. He turned and regarded the big man.

"Señor—you spoke of my own trespasses. We will fight later—perhaps after Hernando has been—disposed of?"

Gardia shook his head, drank his wine and refilled the glass. "No, we will not fight at all, Don Juan."

"But, Señor. Hernando has done only slightly more than I—"

"I am aware of this, Señor. As I said before, I know what has transpired in my absence."

"What then?"

Gardia shrugged, staring moodily at the glass in his hand. "Don Juan—you cannot understand all that crosses a man's mind at a time like this—God grant you never have to—but there is more than a quick rush for the swords. Oh—there was a time, the first time this happened—that I thought differently. The second time I wasn't quite so quick, still, I salvaged my honor. This third time, Señor, plus the added years, makes one reflect. And you will be the fourth time. Think you a little of it. The fourth time, Señor." He looked up, watching Juan's face, then lowered his eyes again to the glass in his hands.

"The fourth time, Juan, might as well be the fortieth, do you not see? What then—must I spend my declining years in these flurries with younger men over a woman who is faithless at the heart? Suppose I kill Hernando Vaz, as I expect to—then you as well—God in Heaven!—it won't be the end, but the beginning. As long as I am able, I must go on carrying the espadas to the oak grove behind the corrals and fight men over a woman who will eventually get me killed, and a lot of fools killed first. Do you understand, then, part of what

94

a man reflects on, in this condition?"

Juan nodded. "Si, I understand Señor." He didn't know how close he dared come to telling Don Francisco what his own conclusions were regarding Elena Gardia, so he said no more.

Gardia didn't speak again for a moment, then he leaned back, put his glass on the table and looked over at Juan. "Besides. Don Juan—there is something else. too, that you don't know about."

"And that?"

Gardia shrugged again. "It is simple. Look you—remember when I left you yesterday on the oak knoll?" Juan nodded. "Well—I detoured so as to pass San Diego Del Carmelo and take the news I carried to our old friend, Don Augustin Perez." A sardonic smile creased the handsome face. "Imagine my surprise, then, Señor, when I almost rode over one of my own Indians crouching in the brush above San Diego Del Carmelo."

Juan stiffened, recalling what Elena had told him of placing San Buenaventura neophytes to spy him out. He nodded, still silent.

"Well—it took nothing more than a word of inquiry, with the quirt dangling from my wrist, to find out what he was doing there."

Gardia's hands lay clenched in his lap, the sole eternal indication of his inner suffering. "You can imagine the rest, Don Juan. I waited until after—she—had ridden out, then followed her."

"It was you, then, Don Francisco—last night?"

"You saw me? Why didn't you—?"

"I never did see you, exactly. When I was riding back to San Diego Del Carmelo, I heard a horseman riding in the night."

"Oh? Well—I was returning then. Going back

homeward."

"And you—where had you been?"

"Señor," Don Francisco said heavily, with a tincture of bitter mirth in his voice. "I was behind the wall where you and my wife talked."

For the second time within his recent recollection, the air pumped out of Juan's lungs in something nearly like a silent gasp. He had the distinct sensation of having goose-flesh under his shirt and along his arms as well.

"Well—Señor, then you have the best proof in the world of what I think of your wife."

"Indeed, Señor, I have, and that is exactly why I refuse to fight you over her."

"Because of what I said, then?"

"Partly, Juan. Mostly, though, because of the absolute truth of those things. I rode by the circuitous routes back to San Buenaventura. A man needs to be alone now and then, as you know. I found that thinking came amazingly easy in the moonlight. There was much thought given into the words you spoke to her. Much thought. I too, reflected. My conclusions were like this; you are a healthy young man suffering the deprivations of our society and yet you were firm and honorable. Also, you are a wise man, as I knew you were the night we met at the fiesta. The more I think of what you told her, the more correct I see that you are, in this instance." Gardia arose, rubbed his hands down the great girth of his massive legs, and nodded at Juan. "That is precisely why I refuse to duel you."

Juan arose, his emotions were tangled in a skein of bewilderment. He wagged his head slowly back and forth. "I should be grateful, Señor, I suppose, for I grant myself to be no match with you over swords; pistols, I will argue about, but not swords—still, again, I must

96

think this thing out."

Don Francisco nodded. "Of course, Señor. You will have until dawn tomorrow morning. I can rely on your presence, then?"

"Of course. I have no choice."

"And I presume you are standing behind Hernando's promise to appear?"

"I am, of a certainty. I have known Hernando Vaz for several years. The thing that most impressed me from the outset, was his complete and iron zeal in maintaining his word of honor. He will be here, Señor, never doubt. Even if he lost a leg, he would still be here."

Gardia made a wry face. "Let us hope such a misfortune doesn't befall him."

Juan resolved on a final effort. "Don Francisco, is there nothing I can appeal to you through, in this instance? Don Augustin? Señorita Carmen, whom I am to marry shortly? Nothing?"

Gardia shook his head. "I am sorry, Juan Martin. As I have already told you. I am ill with the shame of the whole thing. Not just Vaz's shame and my own, and my wife's—but with the necessity of killing him as well." He stopped and regarded Juan in mild surprise. "Marry? You said you were going to marry Señorita Carmen Perez, Señor?"

"Si, it is planned. I forgot to tell you that is another reason for the fiesta at San Diego Del Carmelo, commencing day after tomorrow to be held jointly as a celebration of our leave taking."

"You—will still ride with me, then?"

"Of course, Señor—have Pico and Castro held to their animosity in the face of more imminent dangers?" Juan shook his head. "Neither should we, Don

97

Francisco."

"Mother of God!" The big man said, suddenly, with no attempt at controlling the emotion in his voice. "Go then, Juan Martin. Go with God. We will meet again tomorrow morning."

Juan went. The sunlight was blinding, although Fall had come to the gracious land, and little gouging fingers of brilliance pried in behind Juan's eyes as he rode toward San Diego Del Carmelo, and made him squint against the shimmering heat waves.

The day was well gone when he arrived in the yard and turned his horse back in to the remuda. He turned away, hesitated, and scanned the silla vaqueras that were draped in the shade astride a smooth, gray log. Hernando's was there, among the others. He went slowly toward the house, dreading a meeting with either Augustin or Carmen, his mind going over a plan he had thought of several days before, and shrinking away from it as well.

Head down, he was almost to the wide veranda when a sixth sense made him glance up. The surprise was instantaneous and sharp. Augustin Perez, with the inherent grace and breeding of his race, was being hospitable, although Juan could tell by the bow of his old back, that he was both angry and indignant.

There were two men seated with the old Colonizer. That was Juan's shock. They were both Americans. Sunburned almost to the shade he, himself, was, and resembling Californians in coloring, but their dress was unmistakable. Juan forgot his other troubles at these new arrivals at isolated San Diego Del Carmelo.

Augustin fired a staccato burst of angry Spanish at him when he came up. "These—mataperros—wish to speak with me. Devil of a devil, Juan, they can neither speak

98

Spanish nor I English! What manner of men are these, then, who would come to another land without bothering to learn its tongue, indeed?"

Juan felt the ghost of a smile hover around his mouth at the old man's apparent great disgust—and latent curiosity as well. He nodded to the Americans, saw their intense, surprised looks, and introduced himself. The older of the young men, a rangy, blue-eyed Yanqui with a long, dolorous face and a fierce mustachio designed to break up this angularity, waved a gloved hand toward the other man, a short, burly man with cold eyes but a humorous mouth.

"Mister John Greeley. John's a scout for the Army." Juan nodded coldly, then faced the long faced man again. "I," the latter said in the same, drawling, slightly nasal tone. "am Absalom Reilly."

"Well, gentlemen, what can we do for you?" Juan was amazed at the difficulty he had speaking English. It was as though his mind thought in Spanish, making interpretation into English a laborious, hazardous chore that put the words in improper alignment. It annoyed him a little, too.

Reilly offered Juan a cigar, which was refused. He accepted the rebuff with a fatalistic shrug. "We're going south. There's going to be fighting there before long. Gen'l Kearny's comin' across the damned desert. We figured he'd need every hand he can scare up."

"You are local men," Juan asked. "Rancheros, perhaps?"

"Well—we got grants farther north. Not local, exactly but—"

"You have Mexican grants?"

"Yes, both of us have 'em. We got 'em about two—"

"And you took the oaths of allegiance and

citizenship—to Mexico, gentlemen?"

"Hell yes," Greeley said, testily. "No other way to get the goddamned land."

Juan nodded, letting his antagonism show. "And now you are going south to fight against the Californians?"

Both of the Yanquis closed their mouths tightly, looking up at him where he leaned against the wall above them.

Juan nodded his head gently. "I also have a grant; gotten the same way you got yours. The difference is gentlemen, my word means something to me."

"You aren't going to help Kearny, then?"

Juan made a dour smile. "Well—yes, in a sense. I'm going to help the Californios drive him back where he is at least welcome, if you wish to refer to that as helping him."

Neither man spoke for a while. They both regarded him with frank hostility.

Juan glanced over their heads at Augustin, who was groping for a word, here and there, that he might understand, and becoming more irascible as the seconds went by.

"Is that all you came to San Diego Del Carmelo for, gentlemen?"

They both arose. Greeley looked downright belligerent, although he was acquiring no little respect for the breadth of Juan's chest and shoulders, the more he studied him.

But it was Absalom Reilly who finally spoke. "Well—not exactly. We need fresh horses. Our's are about wore down. Goddamn hot, riding fast, these days." The man's intent blue eyes wavered from Juan's face for a second, then went back to the gray eyes again. "I don't expect, though, you'd care to give us any—

100

now."

Juan smiled thinly. "It's a strange thing, gentlemen, that we have never had horse stealing among us, isn't it? North of us, East and South, the American law is busy hanging horse thieves by the hundreds. Can you find an analogy for the different ways of life there? I can, easily. In California, if you need a horse, you have but to ask and are given one, or, failing that, you can help yourself from the range, for all the horses are branded. You have but to turn the animal loose when you get to the end of your trip, and, eventually, he will be returned." He shook his head. "We have many other things similar, gentlemen. You and your Kearnys want to change all that—well—I don't suppose we can stop you, but I feel we should. For that reason, among others, and my word of honor to support Mexico in return for her generosity, we will oppose one another, if we ever meet again."

Greeley was thoughtful and uncomfortable. It was easy to tell by the flush of his face and the way he looked away, out over the open land as far as one could see. But it was dogmatic Reilly who spoke, first.

"And the horses, Señor—do we get 'em, or don't we?"

"Certainly you get them, hombres. Go to the San Diego Del Carmelo remuda and help yourself. Take good horses, too, friends," Juan added dryly, "for there's a damned good chance the next time you take animals out of someone else's corrals—after you've made the land over—you'll stretch a damned rope for your pains!" He turned abruptly away, showing his back to both of the men, and reciting what each had said to Don Augustin. The Yanquis went quickly down across the yard toward the corral full of horses, sheepish and discomfited.

101

Augustin listened closely, then glared after the men and swore in the vitriolic, vividly descriptive Spanish of generations ago, scorching the men, their antecedents, and the very boards that made their cradles.

They went inside and parted, Don Augustin shaking his head like a worried terrier and ambling toward his counting room, while Juan went in search of Carmen.

She was sewing by the mellow, late sunlight when he went out onto the patio. She smiled up at him with eyes that literally shone.

"Well—caballero mio—what is the news, now?"

His heart was like lead. He had no stomach at all for telling her of the duel. Especially when he wasn't certain, yet, that it would take place.

"Nothing much of any great moment, except that I love you more with each passing hour—minute; second even."

"No?" She said wryly. "I'm sure that's all you know—except for the other things. Come, vaquero— what of Don Francisco and—Hernan'?"

"I can't, truthfully, answer that yet. Please— querida—don't press me until tomorrow for an answer."

She let the stuff in her hands drop slowly, forgotten, into her lap and stared at him. "There is to be a duel, then, Juan—tomorrow?"

"Carmencita," he protested. "There is a good chance that nothing will come of this. Please, then, my love— let it be until I can say with some certainty, won't you?"

"If you wish, my Juan," she said, looking down at the sewing again. "But—I am not deceived, either, you know."

"Chihuahua!" He exploded exasperatedly. "Sometimes I think this uncanny perception of yours is—well—maybe inspired by one of these devils, too."

She smiled and shook her head. "No, I think not. In the first place, Don Juan—my heart—I do not use it like Elena Gardia uses her—attractions."

"No," he complained. "But you surely bedevil a man with it."

"You are angry. Juan?" She was looking into his eyes with that same appeal she had always used on Hernando Vaz. Looking and saying nothing. Juan felt himself under the same spell that had always worked Hernando out of his tirades by the same, appealing, fascinating means of silent glances. He shrugged wryly, and smiled at her.

"Angry? At you? Impossible, Carmen. But—it's just that the—the—tension, is appalling, on one's back."

"I know. You are a great man, Juan Martin. A noble one."

"Nothing of the sort," he put in hastily, feeling extremely uncomfortable and thinking of his scenes with Elena Gardia.

"Oh—but you are. I'll tell you why. You made an error, a pleasurable error, and refused to make the same error again. It takes a certain hardiness of soul to be like that. And you—"

"Carmen—caramba!—just kiss me, will you? Right now I have a great need for this and nothing else."

She put down the sewing and kissed him. Pulled him against her fiercely and kissed him again, until they were both red in the face, then she released him, gave him a brusque push away, and turned back to her handwork, as scarlet cheeked as an apple. He was puzzled by the monumental embarrassment and was going to comment on it, when someone cleared their throat in the archway. He started where he sat and swung quickly, saw Augustin's bright, startled eyes with their sly humor, and felt his own blood mounting in steady waves all the way up into his hair.

"Señor!"

"Excuse me, children. God is my witness; I had no intention of—of interrupting. Dare I advance, now?"

Juan couldn't resist it. He laughed. The tension was instantly broken. Even Carmen darted her grandfather a dry smile, then avoided his eyes as he entered the room and sat down.

"The marriage," he said blithely, "Juan—you must practice for it."

"Is it so complicated, Señor?"

Augustin shrugged, throwing a glance at Carmen. "When I was married, things went on interminably. It seems the good fathers are not content to bind you, amigo. They must also give you a good start toward your goal with infinite advice and endless guidance." He shrugged. "Perhaps times have changed then, who knows? I have sent for Father Salazar from Santa Barbara. He will stay with us until this thing is done with."

Carmen looked at Juan with a mischievous twinkle. "Know you, Don Juan, that we won't meet again until we are married, after tonight."

"Why?" Juan asked in astonishment.

She laughed at him. "It is the custom—imbecile."

"Oh." He looked ruefully at Augustin, saw the concealed desire to laugh in the old man's eyes, and smiled his resignation. None of them spoke until Don Augustin began to make one of his small cigarettes again.

"Juan—you have seen Hernan'? He returned some time ago." He labored with quick, birdlike movements over the corn husk and tobacco. "He seems to be taking this all very well."

Carmen was watching her grandfather's hands. "You told him we are marrying?"

"Si, of course."

"What did he say?"

Augustin shrugged. "It seems I have been in error for some time, children. Hernando was pleased. Of course, he showed a little restraint—I attribute it to shock more than anything else—but still, he was evidently greatly pleased."

Juan nodded silently, blankly, wearing a stony expression and avoiding Carmen's eyes, which he felt on his face.

Augustin fought with a reluctant candle from a niche in the wall, cursed under his breath until the thing was lighted, then inhaled on his cigarette before he sat down with them again.

"Juan—have you any idea when Don Francisco's force will ride?"

"I talked with him this morning, but it slipped my mind."

"Indeed?" Augustin said with some asperity and surprise. "Are you then, not going with them?"

"Certainly, Señor. We talked of other things, I can surely be forgiven this oversight. Anyway, Don Francisco will be here for the fiesta."

Carmen was watching him. "You told him of our wedding?"

"Yes. He was glad to hear of it, little one. He will be here." They were both wondering about Elena Gardia, without knowing the other was doing so.

Augustin smiled and nodded. "Well—it is a certainty that you will ride shortly thereafter, don't you believe?"

Juan nodded. "I am sure of it, Don Augustin. At first,

Don Francisco thought this celebration was for the departure. This indicates, naturally, that we will be leaving soon."

Augustin smoked in silence for a moment, then looked up with a pinched expression of grim pleasure. "Would to God I was also riding against these puercos. Juan—I have had the finest horse of Rancho San Diego Del Carmelo selected and groomed for you. Also, at no little cost I have procured your arms as well,"

Juan had completely overlooked these accouterments he would need. "But, Señor—"

"No, no, amigo—if you please! As I once reminded you, we old ones derive pleasure from small things. Surely you wouldn't deprive us."

He looked at Carmen with a wistful grin. "What can I do, Señorita, to repay such generosity?"

"That's simple, Señor. Marry me off his neck. That alone should suffice to make his last years everlasting."

Augustin snorted, then laughed. They all joined in. Juan alone had to force it a little. The sudden void that was looming ahead of him, after he left this household and this girl he loved, was brought home to him in true proportions, at that exact instant. It was the cradle of an exquisite sadness. He looked at Carmen, saw the same thing mirrored in her face. It hurt him in the heart, but he knew she wouldn't let him see her own agony, ever, so he hid his own. It was wiser, if not less agonizing, that way.

CHAPTER 7

JUAN SLEPT LIKE A LOG FOR THE FIRST SIX HOURS OF the night. His body was exhausted from the strain, but his mind seethed with problems, and finally, in the chill of lateness when the moonlight swelled majestically, blanketing the earth in a softness all its own, he awakened and lay staring out at the ghostly land with its interspersing of dark clumps that were live oaks.

He thought of Hernando down the corridor a little ways, in his own room. The plan he had conceived was little to his liking. Still, desperation drives a hard bargain. It was still several hours from dawn, when they were due at Rancho San Buenaventura.

Reluctantly he pushed back the coverlets and dressed himself. The bowl of water sufficed for a quick toilet, then he went down the gaunt, gloomy corridor until he came to Hernando's room and pushed inside with scarcely a sound, saw the lumpiness of the bed, dropped the tranca back into place on the inside of the door and went over to the small bench where the vaquero's clothes lay in casual indifference, heaped and dangling. He sought deliberately for the poniard, found it by the silvery sheen of moonlight and tossed it into a far corner.

Hernando's breathing was undisturbed. Juan pulled up a bench before he tapped one exposed, richly muscled, rippling dark shoulder. Hernando woke, turned quickly on one elbow and peered belligerently at the intruder.

"You! Holy Mother! Like a ghost. Am I to have no peace then, meddler? Isn't it bad enough that you told Francisco Gardia about me? Aren't you satisfied?" He was awake and angry all at once, proving that his sleep hadn't been as restful as it appeared to be. "You have come to taunt me, hombre?" He made a curt movement towards the disarray of his clothing.

"Hold, fool!" Juan exclaimed tartly. "I didn't come to

taunt you, exactly."

"What then—meddler?" Hernando asked, letting his arm drop but not his eyes. "Is it time to ride? Time to kill this old bull with the heavy conscience who was once a swordsman?"

Juan sat back on the bench, looking at Hernando's powerful back and shoulders. He shook his head. "No, not that either—imbecile." He hesitated over a choice of words, then shrugged away his inhibitions with a curse in Spanish.

"I have come to save your worthless hide."

Hernando looked astonished. He said nothing for a moment, then laughed harshly and made a bitter face. "You—who condemned me to Don Francisco—you would save my neck? Why? Because of a conscience, hombre?"

"No—because of Carmen and Don Augustin."

"Carmen—well—marry her and welcome. I marveled that you could imagine the heart of her being as great as Elena Gardia's, when Don Augustin told me tonight—last night—of the coming marriage. I still marvel. Well—what do you propose, hombre? Running?"

Juan shook his head and arose from the bench. For a moment he stood over the vaquero, then he stooped quickly and his left hand was a blur of movement with an opened palm racing downward in a slashing movement. The sound, when the hand connected with Hernando's face was not unlike a small pistol being fired.

"That—hombre—is to awaken you. I didn't tell Don Francisco a thing. You won't believe it, fool, but Elena Gardia herself told him of your whereabouts. Who else could—idiot—no one—because no else knew where you were!"

Hernando's eyes were glazed in a surge of fury and astonishment. The blow jarred any remaining drowsiness from his mind like one sweeps away cobwebs. He sprang from the bed and rummaged with crazed fingers for the dagger among his clothing. A steady stream of cursing ripped back over one tawny shoulder, then, guessing the truth, he whirled with a mighty oath and threw himself at Juan Martin.

The moonlight made a macabre background for the antagonists. Juan turned sideways a little to meet the onslaught, feeling gray and dismal all over. He knew Hernando Vaz, without his dagger and left to rely on his hands, was no match for him. Californios didn't fight with fists. They considered fighting like that menial, like animals; held it in disdain and disgust.

Juan read the rancor in Hernando's face, flushed and contorted, and had no heart in this fight.

At a disadvantage, Hernando's fury didn't overcome his canniness, however. When he went in his fists lashed out low, hoping to escape Juan's guard. The accuracy of the blows devised was unimpeachable, just the delivery was awkward and inexperienced. Once, swinging high overhand, clubbing with one powerful arm, Hernando was caught in Juan's guard. Their arms met and Vaz staggered forward, almost losing his footing. Juan could have smashed his jaw then, but he didn't. He just moved back and fired a short, sturdy blow that made Hernando go sideways and come up with a throttled roar of rage.

Juan stepped in quickly, then, after Hernando had straightened up, and lashed out with a prodigious blow that slammed into Hernando's chest, jarring him backward where he teetered, then, fully aroused to battle, Juan bore in flailing, twisting his fists into the flesh, feeling it tear under his raw knuckles, before he aimed a vicious coup de grace that blasted like a thundering battering ram into Vaz's averted face, crumbling with gigantic force against the vaquero's head in such a way that his neck couldn't sustain the impact and let his head snap crazily sideways.

Hernando fell solidly, rolled like wet dough and lay still, the spray of blood from his battered nose and mouth making little bloody, bubbly sounds.

Juan sucked air into his lungs to steady himself. There were black and white lines across his vision. He sat down, adjusted his clothing and surveyed the wreckage that was Hernando Vaz. After ten minutes of just resting, he got up, washed himself carefully at the basin-stand, gathered up the rest of the water and threw it on Hernando. The downed vaquero didn't move. Juan went over, knelt and studied his hands and arms. Both showed ample swelling and abuse. Juan was satisfied, arose wearily, got more water and poured it ruthlessly over Hernando's head until some small indications of returning consciousness showed in twitching muscles and groping, blind fingers that felt along the slippery floor.

Juan watched the hands from where he sat. His breathing had returned to normal. Now, there was nothing more he could do until Hernando came round.

The chill that crept into the room made Juan's clothing feel clammy. He wasn't conscious of the perspiration under his jacket until just before Hernando sat up, looking stupidly around himself and probing the damage to his face with sensitive fingers.

"Get up, Hernando. It's time to go."

For a long time Hernando said nothing, nor moved. He regarded Juan Martin with a look of abstract recognition, then he got up slowly, painfully, gasping through clenched teeth at the stitch in his chest where the blow that had really whipped him, had landed.

Juan threw him a towel, poured water into the basin and motioned toward it. The silence was long and insidious. It crept into each man as the seconds went by and became embedded there. Hernando turned to his clothing and dressed with clumsy, badly lacerated and swollen hands. It was a painful ordeal that made Juan's jaws bulge against his locked teeth. But the effervescence of youth was replenishing his energies and by the time Juan lifted the tranca and jerked his head outside, Hernando Vaz was reasonably recovered from his terrific beating.

They saddled horses together in the same, bulky silence, swung up and rode northwest, toward San Buenaventura. A long way off a cougar screamed. The horses lifted their heads in uneasiness and flicked their ears back and forth. The men paid no heed and rode like ghosts, determined, silent and erect in their saddles.

Juan thought of the things they had done together and winced from more vivid recollections of their recent difficulties. He felt nothing beyond apathy towards his one time friend; apathy and a sort of grim resolve to save a life that was racing toward destruction, self willed and certain. It wasn't possible for him to feel any different. A stout heart cannot forget friendship and good times together, so easily. There was no hatred in Juan, for Hernando Vaz. Not even dislike. Just an apathy based on the vaquero's stubborn refusal to see what was being made up out of his infatuation for the magnetic Gardia woman.

Juan's thoughts went to Elena, then. It was a natural thing, for again, a stout heart cannot condemn so readily the excesses that have also brought ecstasy to people carried away in the furious flush of perfect, robust health.

He hadn't seen her since the night that Don Francisco had followed them to the oak knoll. He thought of the way she had betrayed Hernando Vaz to her husband and wagged his head. Perhaps that would convince the vaquero of her faithlessness. He shrugged. Having mentioned it once, back in Hernando's room, it hadn't even brought a reply. Still, he could try again; they were close to San Buenaventura.

"Hernando—can't you see that only two people knew where you were hidden? You and one other—the one who hid you there and sent you food? Are you then, so blind, hombre, that you can't understand it was Elena Gardia herself who gave your hiding place away to her husband?"

Hernando didn't answer right away. He rode along, eyes straight ahead, evidently searching out the landmarks of the big rancho. Then, when Juan was turning away, confident he wasn't going to answer at all, he spoke.

"Maybe she told you, Juan Martin. Conceivably she told you and you told Don Francisco. That's possible, you know."

"No, it isn't. Listen to me. I haven't seen her since we met on the oak knoll night before last. Furthermore, Don Francisco had followed her there. He was behind the wall when I talked with her."

Hernando's head swung slowly, letting his gaze rest on Juan's face in skepticism. Juan noticed in pity how the features were swollen badly where the nose was cracked and the lips split in several places.

"Then—if Don Francisco heard you two talking. why didn't he make himself known?"

Juan shrugged. "I can't answer that. Maybe it was because Elena sought the meeting, had San Buenaventura Indians watch San Diego Del Carmelo until I rode out, then carry her word of my direction so she could catch me. Perhaps it was that fact that his wife, not I, sought this rendezvous, that held his hand."

"He told you he listened?" Juan nodded. "And you knew from what he repeated, that it was so?"

"Absolutely. He was telling the truth."

"You didn't touch her?"

"Not once. Furthermore, I told her things that infuriated her. She threatened to expose you to Don Francisco."

"Why? Because you threatened her also?"

"No, I didn't threaten her, Hernando. I refused to see her any more—and—I think she guessed Carmen and I are in love. At any rate, she was like a mad woman, with her actions and tongue both."

Hernando's voice was thick and drowsy when he spoke again after a prolonged silence that put them near enough to see the massive shadows of San Buenaventura. "It is hard to believe, Juan Martin. Just one thing bothers me. It is this single glimmer of truth that acts like a wedge. It was our secret where I hid. Elena's and mine. Even the Indio never left his shack. I couldn't tell anyone where I was, naturally, therefore, as you say, she had to. Whether she told you or Don Francisco doesn't make much difference. The very fact that she told one of you—both enemies now—is sickening to me. She had to know the result."

Juan nodded to himself. Hernando's reasoning hadn't been exactly what he attempted to inspire, but its goal had been the same and that alone mattered. Now, there was this doubt, finally, in Hernando's mind, and Juan

113

was grateful it had come there, even at this late stage.

He reined his horse past the silent buildings, seeing the deserted, silent appearance of the yard, and went on toward the network of pole corrals where horses pricked up their ears at the approach of the two riders and froze motionless, catching the strange smells of them.

There was a hurricane lantern on the ground near some scrub oaks. Dimly Juan could make out huge, shimmering shadows of incredible length and thinness, standing a little in front and to one side of the light. He rode toward the spot, recognized the mayordomo first, by the shadowed places on his face that were small, sunken pock marks. The light shone from below the flat planes of his face giving him an indescribably evil look.

Don Francisco Gardia was swathed in a black cloak. Juan swung down, let the mayordomo take his horse, and bowed stiffly toward the hacendado. Gardia's cloak, when he returned the bow, filled out voluminously, adding to the eeriness of the scene. Juan glanced at the lantern. It alone among them looked real. The rest were like disembodied spirits. His eyes fell on a square white cloth that lay at the base of the nearest tree, and the two short, sturdy swords that were reposing there, side by side. The sight fascinated him. He had never fought with a sword and the prospect chilled the marrow in his bones.

Juan had the usual Anglo-Saxon's aversion for steel. He turned, saw Don Francisco leaning forward without moving from where he stood, looking into the shadows at Hernando Vaz. The mayordomo returned from tying their horses and glanced at his employer. Don Francisco said nothing. The silence was beginning to become oppressive when he finally walked over closer and stared. Hernando returned the stare with as much animosity as he could muster.

114

"Sangre de Cristo! Hombre, what happened to you?"

Juan saw words forming on Hernando's swollen mouth and stepped in quickly. "It was a slight difference between us, Señor."

The big ranchero looked from one to the other and back to Juan again. "He wasn't going to keep his word, Señor?" The way he said it sounded bewildered, then the black eyes went back to Hernando, looked again at the ravishes showing purple and sullen in the wavering light, and he shook his head slightly back and forth.

"No," Juan said. "It wasn't that, Don Francisco. It was—just—something personal. As I told you yesterday, Hernando's word is his bond."

"But," Gardia said exasperatedly, making a slashing, angry motion in the cool air with one hand. "Look at him, Don Juan; his face, the way he stands, like an old mare with a broken back—"

"A rib, I believe, Señor. Perhaps more than one, who knows?" Juan shrugged indifferently, watching the big man's face.

"A rib then, Don Juan. Mother of God! Look at his hands. Was it necessary even to beat his hands, Señor? How did you expect him to hold a sword, then, amigo? Holy Mary!"

Francisco Gardia's thick neck was veined heavily on one side. It was more indignation than anger, though. He narrowed his eyes and stared at Juan, gauging the shoulders, the arms and chest. "What in the name of Heaven did you do this with, Señor?"

Juan held out his two hands, palms upward. There was a cold, antagonistic challenge in his eyes but he said nothing. Gardia looked at the hands for a moment before he spoke again, then he threw his head back, glancing down at Juan's face with a cold look.

"Did you believe he had to die so quickly, then, Señor, that you wished to cripple him first?"

Juan shook his head. "The opposite, Señor. I gambled on your honor."

"What then?"

Juan nodded toward the silent Hernando Vaz, who was eyeing them both with a gaping mouth. "Señor— you are an accomplished swordsman. Would you, then, fight a man who, at best, is your inferior, and who, at his worst, is a calf at the matanza?" He shrugged without smiling.

Juan looked beyond Gardia at the ugly, coarse features of the mayordomo and was surprised to see the thin, triumphant smile that creased the man's mouth and showed around his small, wide eyes.

Hernando shuttled his feet uncomfortably, looking from one to the other, then he spoke for the first time. "God in Heaven, Señors, are you going to stand here indefinitely? If so, I've got to sit down. There is a slight disinclination within me to remain forever on my feet." He turned and sought a seat by the tree where the twin sabers lay on the white cloth, eased himself down, leaned back without so much as a glance at the murderous weapons, let his head seek the support of the trunk, and closed his eyes.

Ponderously, like a bull who finds himself beset by annoying hosts of little heel-flies, Don Francisco Gardia looked around. He studied the pale face of Hernando Vaz, turned up so that the feeble light from the sky was reflected off it There were tiny circlets of sweat on the man's forehead and upper lip and his teeth, behind the battered lips, were tightly clenched against the rhythmic beat of his heart that carried pain to every part of his being.

Gardia looked his horror at his intended adversary and marveled that two hands could create such havoc, ruin so completely, a man's will and stamina, and leave so little external indication of the shattered self within. Slowly he turned back, glanced at Juan Martin, unmoving, legs spread and puffy hands dangling at his sides, regarding him owlishly without blinking. Then, out of the corner of his eye, he saw the little lantern still burning and his irritation focused on it as something futile and annoying. He swung his head at the mayordomo.

"Chollo, blow out the accursed little light."

The spell was broken. The overseer moved to obey, darting a victorious smile at Juan Martin, who relaxed a little at a time, feeling easier in the heart but still watching the big man and saying nothing, nor moving.

Gardia slumped inside the cloak and turned squarely to face Juan. "Señor," his voice was speculative now; quietly interested and low. "This was no accident. If I am wrong you will correct me. It comes to me that you have repeatedly begged for this imbecile's life—to me. Is this not so?"

"Quite so, Señor," Juan nodded, watching the handsome features working out the thing in advance.

"And this," with a gesture toward Hernando without looking around, "was deliberately done. Briefly, then, Don Juan—you provoked a quarrel, fought Hernando Vaz with your hands, after the fashion of Yanquis, and deliberately crippled him so that he could neither hold a sword or present an acceptable adversary to me."

Gardia's eyes dropped, went quickly to Juan's hands, saw the torn flesh of the knuckles and the puffy, sore look that made the dark skin angry looking, and he shrugged unconsciously.

117

"You—yourself—are rather battered too, Señor."

Juan shifted his weight. "It is inevitable. Even against a man like Hernando, who's ability with the poniard is indisputable, one must expect some retaliation and injury."

Don Francisco shook his head back and forth again. "Mother of God! It is an amazing thing, this business of using the hands as weapons, is it not? He turned, then, knowing no answer was coming, and stared at Hernando Vaz. "Is he badly hurt, Don Juan?"

"No, not seriously. Within two, perhaps three weeks he will be as good as ever. A scar here and there, conceivably, on his face and hands, but otherwise none the worse."

Gardia nodded thoughtfully. "It was extremely clever of you. Two or three weeks, Señor, is more than ample time for the saving of his foolish soul. Well," he shrugged, threw a glance at the swords on the white cloth and his mayordomo, both of whom were easily seen now that the first rays of daylight were enrichening the land. "Whether I approve of your brutality or not, Señor, is neither here nor there. You have achieved your ends, and that alone is paramount at this time." He waved a hand toward the swords. "Chollo—take them back to the house, if you will."

The mayordomo dutifully wrapped the blades in their soft coverlet, tucked them under one arm, threw a satisfied look at the three men and. stalked off toward the deserted yard where some spindly, voracious chickens were astir.

"Don Juan—my thoughts are in conflict. It isn't so much the saving of this fool, although that rankles a little. It is other things."

"You said, yourself, Don Francisco, you had no taste

118

for this fight anyway."

"Si, I did. Nor was I anticipating it with any relish either. Still—one's honor, Señor, must be satisfied."

Juan shrugged. "Will I do, then?"

"You?" Gardia said with a sardonic smile. "With your hands in that shape? Señor—I want satisfaction—not butchery."

"Well—perhaps I would have difficulty holding a saber, Señor, but there is still my way of fighting. I assure you nothing has injured my fists to the extent I can't use them in this fashion again."

Gardia looked at the steady gray eyes with a faint, downward twist of his mouth. "That, as you know, is the same as dog-fighting. Besides," the mouth twisted wryly upwards a little, in dry appreciation for the disadvantage to such a fight, "I know nothing of this combativeness."

"Nor I—nor Hernando—Señor. "An impasse, then. A very cleverly worked out impasse. I respect your ability to think so well, ahead, Don Juan."

Juan shrugged. "And now—Señor Gardia?"

"Who is to say? One must think. This is awkward. Unthought of, even."

Juan stirred from his place for the first time since their arrival. He turned abruptly and went over beside Hernando Vaz, and knelt, looking at the greenish tint around the man's mouth.

"Hernando?"

"Si—what is it?"

"I want you to ask Don Francisco who told him where you were hiding, on Rancho San Buenaventura."

"Volgame Dios! I am not interested."

Juan saw the shadow loom up at his side and glanced up. The hacendado was standing there, gazing down in shock at the face made more repugnant in the naked

119

light. "Tell him, Señor, who it was who disclosed his hiding place to you."

Francisco Gardia reflected in silence for a time, then nodded shortly, brusquely. "My wife, Señor Vaz. She told me of this treachery of yours after I had followed her home from another tryst."

Hernando opened his eyes and looked stonily at the ranchero. This tryst, Señor. Was it at Don Juan's oak knoll?"

"It was."

Hernando looked at them both. Naturally, Gardia was speaking the truth. He had to be. What possible reason could any man have to admit his wife was a villainess, when he proposed no action as a result of it? He fought back the certainty of Elena's indifference to his fate with a physical effort. He wanted to groan aloud. One lie, under the circumstances, was a little wedge that pried apart far down in the dungeon of despair, watching the unfolding of the entire tragedy that kept spreading wider and wider, becoming blacker and deeper, when Juan spoke. He heard the words and understood but made no move, for a long while, to obey them.

"Hernando, get to your horse and ride back to San Diego Del Carmelo." Juan saw the blankness of the eyes. He saw a faint flicker of understanding in them and got to his feet, leaned forward to brush the dust from his knees, then straightened and walked a little way aside. Francisco Gardia followed him, the great cloak looking slightly ridiculous, now, in the full light of early morning. Horses neighed in the near distance and an old dog barked whiningly at some Indian's shack.

"Don Francisco, I would like to speak my mind. I readily concede, Señor, that in many things I have overstepped the bounds of propriety. I don't ask you to believe I did these things in order to avert what I saw coming—yet I did. And I'll not say the rewards were altogether satisfactory, either. Just one thing still bothers me, Señor."

"And that, Don Juan?" The big man's eyes seemed no longer disturbed over Juan's brutality toward Hernando or the reason for it. Instead, there was a respect—even leaning—toward Juan Martin. Gardia was a man's man in all things. He could understand courage, manliness and clear thinking, far easier than he could comprehend the intricate workings—machina-tions—that had nearly cost someone their life as a result of his wife's infidelity and cruelty.

"Doña Elena, Señor—what of her?"

The ranchero shrugged, let his gaze wander over Juan's shoulder to the big house of Rancho San Buenaventura. There was a hardness to the glance, a subtlety, that Juan had never suspected in Francisco Gardia. It reminded him of the archness he had been surprised to find in Carmen, that afternoon on the patio, when she had told him of her love. This was different, though. It was like steel in the sunlight. Hard and cold without emotion.

"Don Juan—I have given this much thought, as you will appreciate. Much thought."

Juan ran an incalculable risk, then, but he insisted that the blame be placed where it belonged for the barely averted tragedy to San Diego Del Carmelo, Rancho San Buenaventura, and all those who inhabited both places, plus the stigma of shame to every name and family involved.

"You will forgive my bluntness, Señor. If you think I speak beyond the realm of decency, knowing—or

121

presuming—on the fact that we cannot fight, should I outrage your honor just remind me of it. I'll apologize and withdraw."

Gardia made a motion with one hand "Don Juan, what can you say to me, now, that could infringe on my honor? After what we have been through these past two days, God knows there should be small consideration of pride between us, then, hombre."

"Then," Juan said coldly. "I fasten the blame, Señor, where I am convinced it belongs."

"On my wife, of course," Gardia said without removing his eyes from the distant house.

"On your wife," Juan repeated. "I ask nothing but logic. I neither condemn her nor accuse her to you. I ask only that you consider the thing from the start. True, there is some that you don't know. Ask then, perhaps I can fill in the missing pieces."

Don Francisco shook his head slowly. "No. It is of small importance. The details are unimportant, we both know this. The scope of this—thing—Señor, isn't necessary in arriving at the causes or the ultimate. I agree with you, in spite of the grief it causes me."

Juan, seeing the steely black eyes with no hint of remorse or sadness in them, just melancholy and resignation, doubted very much if Don Francisco Gardia was capable of feeling anything akin to grief at all, for his spirit was that of a bear or a lion, capable of being outraged, angered and aroused, but only in the channels which he considered worthy of a man. The delicacy, or finesse, of any situation would pass unnoticed, only the hard core of reality would remain to be sifted and evaluated.

He longed to ask what was in Don Francisco's mind but shrank from such an overt intrusion. He had already

122

said more than he should, in placing all the blame on Elena. He looked away from the man's face, saw even a whit of pity for Elena Gardia in this moment of Hernando's slumped, lolling form on his horse, riding back toward San Diego Del Carmelo. If there had been her travail, it was lost at the sight of the shamed, broken rider going back homeward. He recalled Carmen's words, one time, about how Elena would give her back Hernando Vaz, to breathe a new soul into, and inwardly marveled at the insight that had let Carmen see, so perfectly and clearly, where this affair would end.

He felt gratitude, too, for surely, having seen so far ahead, surely Carmen would also have considered the best and most efficient way to do what was her duty, to Hernando, if not exactly her obligation.

His thoughts were interrupted by Francisco Gardia. "Señor—I'm sorry this meeting ended in such a— fiasco. Still, perhaps it is better this way, in a sense. At any rate I offer my thanks for your interest and consideration, and bid you adios."

Juan bowed silently and stepped aside. The ranchero strode past with no expression showing on his face. He watched him go, wondered if San Buenaventura would still be represented at the fiesta, shrugged and went over to his horse, mounted and followed Hernando Vaz's circuitous route around the rancho yard and southwest, back toward San Diego Del Carmelo.

CHAPTER 8

THE COMMISSION OF ANY ACT OF VIOLENCE REQUIRES an intellectual acumen and poise that no one possesses when they are upset enough to commit such an act.

This was borne home to Juan during the wedding ceremony. He was painfully conscious of the lacerated condition of his hands and knew that others had noticed also. Carmen, beside him, kneeling, had said nothing beyond inquiring if, perhaps, he hadn't fallen with his horse. He knew, from the quiet way she said it, that she didn't believe it for a moment, but, gratefully, he had accepted it and allowed it to be circulated without correction.

The ceremony was tedious in the extreme. He had a hard time keeping his mind from wandering. There was perspiration against his back and chest as well, neither of which made him any more inclined to appreciate the affair at all. When it was over and the congratulations were in process, he had to smile each time his sore hands were grasped although he felt like anything but registering pleasure, right then. Even the Californian custom of great, loud humor, bounced off him like leaves falling in the late autumn, which it was then, too. But he bore it all stoically, even forcing a sally or two of his own, until they came to the end of the line and Carmen went one way, with some distant female relation, and old Augustin took him in tow, leading the way to the counting room.

As he left the throng of people, the music started with evident impatience to overcome the funeral atmosphere that had preceded.

Augustin poured them both wine, said a very sincere and solemn toast and kept his eyes on Juan's face as they drank. "You will excuse me, Juan, if I call you son. Surely, grandson, aside from being awkward, doesn't fit. It is like this. You are a grave young man, older than your years in the head. This is good, of course, and I am proud that you are made thus. I will call you son, then, with your permission."

Juan bowed without smiling. "As you will, Señor. I confess that I married Carmen as much for you as a father, as to take her for a wife." He had always been very fond of the wispy old hacendado.

Augustin laughed suddenly and poured more wine. His eyes were sparkling. "Well—it wouldn't be wise to say such a thing where the little shadow can hear it." He drank the wine slowly, this time. "One thing, if you will, Juan. Your hands, it was a painful accident, that?"

Juan smiled dryly. "In some ways, yes, Señor. In other ways no."

"Ah? A parable?" He shrugged elaborately. "No matter. Listen to me. I met Hernando this morning just as he was riding out."

"I missed him at the wedding."

"Of course. So did others. I heard some comment on it, but, as I was about to say, I met him this morning and, of all things, he also, had taken a bad fall from his horse; while he was running full tilt too, he said." The black eyes were like shiny beads. They didn't move when the thin shoulders rose and fell. "It is unfortunate that San Diego Del Carmelo horses have suddenly developed this inability to maintain footing on the land they were bred upon, isn't it?"

Juan said nothing, watching the older man's face. Augustin finished his drink, went over slowly, took one of Juan's hands, lifted it, stared, and shook his head.

"Unbelievable."

"What, Señor?"

"Oh—simply that the palms, Señor, are untouched. Just the backs—the knuckles—are injured."' He let the hand drop, went over, looked thoughtfully at the decanter of wine for a moment, then turned back. Juan saw the ironic smile in his eyes. "I had better not—so soon. You know how Carmen is. Still it is excellent wine, is it not?"

"The best in the Californias," Juan said, and meant it.

"And those hands, son, may well be likewise, before all this trouble is over."

"How is that?"

"Like this. The land is troubled badly. Worse, it is divided, which means we cannot win. Together, would be extremely difficult. I know this much because yesterday I drove to Santa Barbara in my buggy. The news is garbled."

"The hands. Señor," Juan reminded him.

"I'm coming to that. The American authorities say they will absolutely uphold all legitimate Spanish and Mexican land grants. There will be disenfranchisement, Juan. Well—all this being true, our cause is lost—in a way—yet, on the other hand, the Americans say conclusively that the British, from over the sea, are closing in on California from up above," Don Augustin waved a hand vaguely northward "Then, amigo, our course must be fixed and definite—altered even, so that we embrace our former enemies. Such things have happened often in my lifetime. Juan—far better that we belong to our neighbors of this continent, than become another dangling appendage to some foreign empire, Mexican or British. Therefore, I ask you not to ride to the war with Don Francisco Gardia, but to stay here, at San Diego Del Carmelo, where you belong, and guide our rancho through the times of adjustment ahead. Now do you understand what I meant by the hands?"

Juan nodded, crossed the room to a wall bench and sank down, still holding his half empty wine glass. "Si. Señor. I thought it was something else you meant."

"That," Augustin said dryly, "is too obvious to comment on. Hernando's face, your hands. It is a sad thing, of course, but—Sainted Mother—I am very humble too."

"Why, Señor?"

"Like I said, I saw Hernan' this morning. He wished me to convey you an apology for something," a wry shrug, "naturally, I didn't inquire. Still, one doesn't live to my age for nothing, son, believe me. He said he was going over to your oak knoll for the day. Perhaps he will return tonight, he didn't say."

"He isn't riding away—is he?" Juan asked with a sinking heart.

Augustin shook his head. "No, I asked the same thing. There are times—you know this, I'm sure—when it is better for a man to be alone a little. Make peace within himself, as it were."

Juan nodded thoughtfully, wishing he could walk out, saddle a horse and ride also to the oak knoll. He and Hernando Vaz had been companions, old friends for so long. It was sad to think of what had happened between them. It could be patched up, conceivably. Juan could think of no reason why not but the scars would always remain. He looked up at Augustin. It was very probable, however, that even the scars would make them closer, later on, when the action turned to reaction.

"Don Augustin—I have thought in my mind. Look you, by your leave, Carmen and I could live at San Diego Del Carmelo. We could build a smaller house on the grounds—somewhere." He watched the old man biting back a flood of words with heroic strength, and paused. Augustin's barriers gave away completely, then.

"I have prayed one of you might come to this. Look you, Don Juan. I have need for so little. Holy Mary! I

127

wished this might happen. It is as God has willed it and I am eternally grateful." He looked askance at the wine bottle again, fought a wavering, losing battle with his resolve, swore a mighty, rusty oath and filled both glasses again with a harassed look over his shoulder. "I ask only small conditions, Don Juan. You must grace this empty house with my great-grandchildren. You must not ride to this lost war, I plead with you. In this, I have experience. I can tell how these things will go. Mother of God! I have witnessed oceans of blood in my time, spilt as fruitlessly, as senselessly. There is one other thing—but I can't suggest it." He studied Juan's puzzled face and sipped his wine before he went on. "It concerns Hernando."

Juan smiled. "Well—what I was about to say before, Don Augustin. If we live here—my wife and I—" the word startled him, "then, wouldn't it be better if Hernando had his own rancho?" He saw the impatient interruptions forming again, but didn't surrender so readily this time.

"Please—I realize my rancho was developed by you of San Diego Del Carmelo But—Señor—we will have little need for more land than is here."

"Exactly!" exploded Augustin. "Exactly! Ah—the Lord is good! You have a good heart, Juan Martin, an old man could ask nothing better in a new relation. Nothing better, indeed."

"That was your other condition then?"

"Well—not my condition, Juan, but my hope."

"It is settled then?"

"Si, it is settled."

Don Augustin arose, set his empty glass down with some reluctance, and smiled. "Juan—a favor. Come with me to the remuda. I wish a horse saddled."

They left the house by the rear exits and crossed the busy yard before Juan spoke. He had a horse brought up for the hacendado, watched the old man mount, then put a hand on his leg for a second.

"Señor? You ride to the oak knoll?

"Exactly."

Juan smiled and rubbed his jaw. "Convey a message for me, if you will."

"My pleasure, Señor."

"There will be another matanza in the Spring. Request of Hernando, his agreement that we rope together again, like in years past."

Augustin said nothing. He put a thin old hand to his poblano, bowed slightly, ran the back of the hand under his nose with a fierce, irritated movement, frowned as he brought it back down, and reined away.

Juan was still watching him lope along like a slim youth of fifteen, straight as an arrow with a back made stiff and proud with the blood of Castile, when someone touched his arm lightly. He looked around and down. Carmen smiled at him.

"He has gone to the oak knoll, mi alma?"

"Si, how did you know?"

"Know!" she said with spirit. "Who, think you, convinced Hernan' that was the best place in the land for a man to reflect in?"

He reached down and touched her shoulder, let his fingers go under her chin, up the smoothness of her throat, then he stooped quickly and kissed her fleetingly and straightened again. "There are times—Señora— when I wonder if, after all, it isn't conceivable for an angel, as well as a devil, to come to earth."

"I couldn't tell you—my husband—but if you'll dance the first dance with me, I'll be glad to spend the

129

rest of the evening—the night, even—talking this over with you."

They went back to the house. The noise was a boisterousness that sent echo after echo over the land, each sound chasing other sounds, and, in turn being pursued with new sounds, until it was a great tumult of human laughter, shouting and music, attesting to the enjoyment of the rancheros and their families.

Juan danced because he enjoyed it, but in the back of his mind was the guilty sensation of not riding with Francisco Gardia, and how he could possibly make the hacendado see his reasons for not riding.

It was exactly as old Augustin had said. If the land was divided, not only against its own loyalties, but against the invaders as well, how could the Californios hope for even a temporary victory? He thought back to the two men—Greeley and Reilly—who had borrowed San Diego Del Carmelo horses, and made a slight face over the recollection. There was a difference, of sorts, in the way men looked at the same thing. There was nothing heroic about deliberately staying away from where your loyalties lay, whether they were nebulous or actual ones. Also, there was nothing courageous about betraying your word, either, as Greeley and Reilly were doing. And yet, he had this in common with them, he, by abstaining from the conflict, they, by participating. The victory of Yanqui arms was ensured.

He smiled automatically at his partner, the massive Doña Eleanora Dominquez, of Rancho Soledad, and thought to himself, of the two, his own role was the least savory. At least Greeley and Reilly were fighting for the thing they believed in, while Juan Martin—John Martin—was, by tacit abstinence, withholding an arm—a lance—from the cause he believed in, although he

130

knew as well as he knew anything, it was foredoomed to failure.

Where, then, did his loyalties lie? He looked around, saw Carmen watching him with wide, black eyes, waited an opportunity to escape and let the dancers whirl by without him. Carmen, as though by telepathy, waited against a far wall, in a shaded, secluded corner, for him to cross the room to her.

He noticed with an abrupt recollection of the exact night and circumstances, that where his wife stood, was the precise spot he had first let his guard down sufficiently for her quick insight to perceive that he cared for her.

"Juan? You are troubled about something. It is in your face, querida; come," she tugged gently at his jacket. He followed dutifully. They went out into the patio where empty wine glasses indicated others had been, and sat down.

"Now, my lover what is it?"

"This confounded war." He faced her with a rueful look.

"What kind of a war?"

They both laughed, then he spoke again, softly. "Carmen—. Have I ever told you that, absolutely, you are the most bewitching female I have ever seen?"

"That doesn't answer my question, although I confess I love the sound of what you say."

"It's an English word; a sort of half-polite swear word."

"It has a counterpart in Spanish?"

"No," he shook his head. "It would be difficult to find one. Don't worry, I'll teach you English soon enough."

"And the war—what of it?"

"Augustin doesn't want me to go. He says—"

131

"We cannot win. I know. But Juan—if you want to go, amour, then by all means go. It is, I think, the desire of every man to be a part of something big, something stirring and historic—something he can point to and say he had a hand in the fashioning of."

Juan looked at her, awed. "Good Lord, you are even more amazing as I get to know you." He was filled with a sense of something close to humility, intermingled with his awe of her. "Tell me something, Señora. How can you know how a man feels? What do you know of them, that you can see inside their souls?"

Carmen's eyes wrinkled into a smile. "Juan—if I answered that truthfully, it wouldn't only dispel your flattering delusion, it would also—possibly—shatter your masculine pride."

"Well, dispel and shatter then, heart of my heart. I want the truth."

She regarded him tenderly. "Because, my Juan, men—all men—are so amazingly simple. The most simple of all, are the young, honest ones. Even when they have old minds, like you have, they are still simple. Look you, querida mia—there was never much doubt in my mind what this Elena Gardia might do to you. I cried into my pillow over it. And yet, I knew as well as I knew we would be married, one day, that you would resist her. Oh, it wasn't because of me—not then—Juan, it was because what she was doing was against the honesty within you, the basic substance of you, my darling. So, you almost stumbled," she shrugged gracefully, forcing her eyes up again, so that he saw the black, opaque softness of them, like liquid. "But that, also, had to happen. You stumbled, but you didn't fall. Hernando fell, Juan, because he is a boy in the mind. You aren't." She stopped talking, sat there looking at him with misty eyes. "I don't make myself clear, I know. Perhaps, some day, when you have taught me English I can express myself better—quien sabe?"

"Not in English, mi amour. In English there isn't even an appropriate word for great sacrifice, for courage and fortitude above normal." He shook his head at her, proud that she, with all her ravishing beauty and intelligence, should be the wife of John Martin, a drifter, a dreamer, perhaps, from the farthest reaches of the continent.

"Well—the truth about you, my love, goes farther than this interlude, this tragedy of the Gardia woman."

"As for the war, possibly?"

"Fully that far Juan—my grandfather spent thirty years with reins and sword in his hand. He is old now, true, but again, honest men are simple creatures. Even in their wars and conquests—of the land, I mean—they are simple. This war is no different. Francisco Gardia, himself, has said many times we are a divided people. That Castro wants annexation to the Estados Unidos, that Mariano Vallejo does also; that Pio Pico does one day, and doesn't the next. Where is the purpose then, my darling, that could bring you anything but suffering, from either defeat or victory? Do you not see that, while I know you wouldn't be killed in this war, I still see no sense in you even going. If there was, Juan in your own mind, a fixed idea on the subject, I would ask you— even ask you, my husband—to go, because always you would feel that you hadn't lived up to what you believe in. But there isn't this determination in you, and we both know it."

"Oh?" Juan said quietly. "And how do *you* know what's in my mind?"

She threw out a hand toward him and let it stay there,

133

three feet from his chest. "Juan—if there was a determination to see victory in you, and the rest of us as well, you wouldn't be here now! You would have ridden away long ago. There is no zeal in any of us, I don't believe, for this fight. Of course there are some vaqueros who ride out for the sheer excitement of it, my Juan, but watch how they'll turn back when others die. They aren't cowards—just men who went for a lark and withdrew when it became something serious they didn't care a fig about. You are no different. In your heart you don't believe California can stand against the Americans—then why die to prove you are both right and wrong?"

Juan was captured completely by her spell. By the fire that looked out of her eyes at him, by the increased respiration, by the very vitalness of her. He said nothing until the silence threatened to grow embarrassing, then he smiled at her.

"I'm more in love with you, after that tirade, than I ever was. Carmen—I have waited too long for you, much too long."

She blushed uncertainly, watching his face. "You—aren't teasing me?"

"Upon my word I mean every word of it."

"Well, then—am I right or wrong?"

"Perfectly right. I have never thought the Californians could whip the United States, and don't think so now. It's just that—well—of the two ways of life, I choose ours. I like it well enough to fight for it, too, sweetheart, and yet—I know the cause is a lost one as surely as Don Augustin—and you—do."

"You knew all this and yet you would fight anyway?"

He saw the puzzled look in her eyes. His smile widened. "That shouldn't bewilder one so apt at reading

134

men, amado, as you are."

"It doesn't Juan. Just tell me one thing. This desire to fight—it was in your mind before you told me you loved me?"

"Yes, before."

"And now?"

He watched the tenseness coming into her face. "And now, my darling, I don't have it. Only a confusion, sort of. A wondering what is the right thing to do."

"You are doing it right now, Señor. Sitting on the patio of Rancho San Diego Del Carmelo, where you belong. Where we both belong. One man with a lance— or a thousand—can't alter destiny. You know this as well as I do, better even; still, if you feel any urging to go out and fight, then you must do so. No woman alive should hold her man back from what is in his mind."

"Well," he said. "I'm not going. There is still the unpleasantness of telling Don Francisco, however, and that looms large in my eyes—and probably in his eyes as well." It was dryly said, with a slight grin.

Carmen shrugged. "He will understand better than you think. He will always understand things of this nature, where—well—things of different natures, like of the heart for instance, he will never understand."

Juan said nothing again. It was wonderfully pleasant on the patio, relaxed and left alone by discreet Californios who understood and sympathized with them.

He recalled his talk with Augustin, concerning the rancho and Hernando. "Carmen—would you rather live here, at San Diego Del Carmelo—or my place?"

"But here, of course. Aside from my own desires, it is also grandfather's wish. He hasn't said so, and never will, but I can see it." She stopped abruptly, looking into

135

his gray eyes, and blushed. "But, of course, you are the master—now."

The sudden repentance made him laugh aloud and shake his head. "You are a fabulous creature. Well—anyway—querida, I told Don Augustin to give my rancho to Hernando. He needs it, we don't."

"Thank God, Juan. I am very glad. Hernan' needs something to settle him."

He thought, suddenly and with no reason, of the two swords on the white cloth under the oak tree and told himself silently that Hernando finally, in the same day, had secured more settling from the present of the rancho, than he would have had with certainly more finality, from Gardia's blades. But what he said was altogether different.

"I haven't seen any of the retinue from San Buenaventura. Don Francisco assured me he would be here."

"And—her?"

"He didn't say. I doubt if she would have the—"

"Yes, she would!" Carmen spat out. "After all, my life, she needs new—new—victims now. The others awakened and left."

"Carmen!"

She wrinkled her nose at him. "I was saying it as Hernan' would have. 'What would you then, for the love of God, a lie'?"

It was a creditable mimicking of Vaz; they both laughed.

"Don Francisco is to ride by with his force. His sixty caballeros. I was to be the sixty-first."

Carmen was wagging her head back and forth before he stopped talking. "I offer you a wager, then, my soul. I make you the wager that has closer to half of those who were to ride with him, than he has of the full sixty."

"And the wager, Señora?"

"Ten kisses on your lips." She didn't blush at all, but Juan was startled by the brazenness of it and showed it the way his eyes widened.

"Well, my husband?"

"I find myself, Señora, wishing with all my heart—even considering ways—to forestall at least one half of Gardia's force by trickery, bribery—anything at all."

She laughed suddenly, flashing white teeth at him, then she cocked her head a little and looked out from under the thickness of her long, curling lashes. "In that case, Señor, I feel bound to pay you in advance—as soon as we grow weary of the fiesta, later."

"Later!" he said vehemently. "But I am tired now. Tired to the death of me, Señora."

Another peal of laughter. "No—not yet, my darling. For appearance sake, if no other, we must not leave too soon."

They arose and stood close, looking into each other's eyes, then Carmen turned away quickly, reddening, and felt for his hand.

"You are worried because the Gardias' didn't arrive, Juan?"

"He said he would be here. Of course, under the circumstances I don't blame him if he doesn't come at all."

"What circumstances?"

"I'll tell you tonight—when we are alone."

"Consider, caballero, there is the possibility that I won't want to take the Gardia's troubles with me, any longer."

"Some other time, then. It isn't important any more."

"But darling," Carmen said, turning a little, waiting

137

for him to move toward the archway, back toward the barbecue and dancing, with her. "Isn't it probable San Buenaventura will arrive tomorrow?"

"Very probably, loveliest of all women. And likely as well."

"Come, then. The jokes are bad enough as it is. If we stay alone a minute longer they will become unbearable."

"Among the women, too?" he asked, aghast.

"But of course." She threw him a taunting glance full of promise and fire. "Juan Martin you have much to learn. I will teach you."

They went back into the bedlam and Juan thought back to similar words said to him not too long before, by another woman. One altogether different from the one who just said them this second time.

CHAPTER 9

THE FIESTA WAS A PROLONGED AFFAIR. UNDER circumstances where the guests traveled many miles in carretas and horseback—only the wealthiest could afford buggies of any kind—and in a land where time was less than dirt and hearts overflowing with the love of life and humanity—Yanquis to some degree excluded—it was natural, then, for the people to lengthen every celebration. There was much to discuss any time, but now, with strife latent, new generations being born that must of a necessity be inventoried by distant relatives, the length of a fiesta might be three days or a week, rarely less.

Along toward morning, most of those less fortified by Augustin Perez's wines—or perhaps because of them—

138

sought beds. Sleeping humanity was everywhere. Only two rooms escaped the invasion. Augustin's own room, and that part of the establishment scrupulously set aside for the newly-weds. But with the breaking of a new day, San Diego Del Carmelo ebbed and flowed with life again, the barbecue pits were stirred back into life, sides of beef were lowered and Indians groaned under the weight of oaken logs.

Horsemen were everywhere. There were endless competitive sports, like the amansadores showing their art at handling unbroken horses, the eminently superior Reindadores with their colts, some with two reins on the jaquima, some with more advanced animals still carrying the jaquima, but being bitted. Carrying the Las Cruces or Santa Barbara spade bits, a few with the rarer ring-bits and half-breeds, competed to see whose horse reined to the lightest touch or whirled, set-up, or backed and turned better.

In one of the larger, newer corrals made exclusively of stout oak logs, the dangerous pastime of coursing a bear was in progress. This consisted, simply, of horsemen teasing a huge California Grizzly until he was raging mad, then letting him fight it out with one of the murderous, crafty long-horned Spanish bulls.

There were constant Coleadas, as well. Horsemen upending a thousand-pound steer by his tail. Anything less than a complete upending was derided as poor showmanship. Then, of course, there was the ancient sport of burying a rooster up to his very wattles in the hard ground, and making bets as to who could charge by in a full, belly-down run, and snatch the hapless bird from his hole by the head. This, as well as the other sports, resulted in some nasty spills, but participant and spectator alike, enjoyed every second of it.

Augustin was drawn aside and made to listen to many allusions to the lateness of the newly-weds in joining the fiesta on its second day. In some, the old Colonizer was highly pleased and laughed as uproariously as the rest, but with other jokes and innuendoes, less subtle, perhaps, his face remained stony and unappreciative.

It wasn't until Juan and Carmen came out, he, pale and wincing in advance of the shout that went up when they appeared, and she, as red as a beet and a thousand times more alluring, that the joking became overwhelming.

It was close to noon before the older ones gave it over, and much longer before the younger ones, especially the caballeros, finally allowed their humor to subside.

Augustin, not as influenced by his fabulous wines as he normally would have been by that time, for the very simple reason that he hadn't gotten up early, having arrived back from the oak knoll very late, collared Juan and Carmen and took them aside.

"Children, poor Hernan'," he darted a fascinated look at Juan's hands, and seeing the apprehension in his granddaughter's eyes. "Well—he will be a day or two late, coming home."

"What then, grandfather? Has he gone somewhere? What is it?"

Don Augustin shot a quick, knowing look at Juan before he answered. "Well—there is, of course, a certain degree of discomfort to being thrown by a—horse. You can understand this—little shadow—but more than that, one must have his wounds looked after."

"Are they *that* bad, grandfather?" Carmen's eyes were large and round. Juan was stirring his feet uneasily, wishing Don Augustin would get it over with.

"Not so awfully bad, querida. Still—he has ridden to Santa Barbara to spend the day there and seek medical advice. It is this internal danger of infection, you must know. These complaints that bother a man, once they gain access to his flesh." He shrugged, stealing another furtive look at Juan's hands. "It is really nothing little shadow, just wise precaution is all. Anyway, he won't be here for the dancing tonight, but, possibly, tomorrow."

Juan was watching Carmen out of the corner of his eye. She nodded, looking at her grandfather, then turned quickly when several girls of her own age came up, giggling, ogling Juan with fascinated, abashed stares, but, before she turned completely to go with them, she flashed one long look at her husband's hands, too. There was an incredible wonderment to her look, altogether different from Don Augustin's stare. It said, quite plainly, that it was beyond comprehension how one pair of hands could be so brutal and yet—also so tender as well.

Augustin waited until Carmen was well out of earshot, then he wagged his head dolefully, looking at Juan. "Holy Mother, caballero! It is unbelievable, this using the hands so. Why—know you, Juan—his ribs are cracked like so many barbecued sides of beef. It is difficult to see where a man would have such tremendous strength." The head still wagged back and forth, awed.

Juan cocked a jaundiced gray eye at his relation by marriage. "Señor, has it occurred to you that this game has two sides?"

"How is this?"

"Look you, in the first place Carmen knows perfectly well what happened to Hernando. She thinks *you* don't

141

know. Perceive? You, on the other hand, think you are sparing her feelings, too, amigo—thus, the game is played by both of you with me—the cause, or maybe I should say the effect—as a very unwilling bystander, standing on pins and needles, as it were."

"Mother of God. I hadn't thought of it quite like that." Don Augustin's face relaxed in thought. Then, very slowly, the humor of it began to pervade him. Almost as though with reluctance, he chuckled, it grew into a chirping sound deep in his throat and stayed like that for a long time, then his head went back and he rocked with laughter. All this Juan watched with sardonic humor, himself.

"'Sta bien, compadre," Juan said when the mirth had died to a high, nasal sound that wasn't unpleasant. "What did Hernando say—if you can spare the breath from your great good joke."

"Peace, Juan, peace." Augustin controlled himself with an effort and wiped at the outside corners of his eyes. "Hernan' was contrite, son." He sobered then, on a sudden indignant recollection. "Know you, Don Juan, that that idiot kept me on the accursed knoll in the chill—at my years, mind you—until nigh two in the morning, by the nearest reckoning."

"But why?"

"He wouldn't accept your rancho. I finally won him over by assuring him through chattering teeth, that he would have murder on his soul for a certainty, if he kept me up on that spot through the entire night, with the cold settling into my meat like poison."

"But—he did agree, Señor?"

"Yes—the imbecile—finally. And Juan—he assured me that there is no one in the entirety of Alta California he would rather rope at a matanza with, than his foster-

142

brother-in-law—is that right, I wonder? Well, no matter—that's you."

Juan sighed his relief. "In the end, then, Don Augustin, all appears to be well. No?"

"But of course. God willed it so."

Juan nodded. "Excuse me, Señor, my wife—"

"Certainly," Augustin said, glancing toward the groaning table where his proud vintage shone like liquid gold in the sunlight. "Of course, after all, Don Juan, your wife was only born here—she most certainly needs your arm to guide her."

Juan turned, startled at the sarcasm where he had never met any before, and stared. Don Augustin's head was going back again as he moved toward the laden table, and the chirping laugh was coming from his mouth. Juan grunted wryly and went among the throng, accepting solid thumps on his shoulders and roguish smiles from the women, while he sought Carmen.

She saw him among the people who were thronged about where she was hemmed in, heaping congratulations on her as only those of Spanish descent can do, and flashed him a pleading look for succor. It took a lot of happy byplay to get her away, but his success was heightened by a new horsemen's sport which was heralded by riders wheeling among the mob.

When they were alone, Carmen looked seriously up at him. "My darling, how can a woman love as I do? It is everywhere, within me. Oh, Juan—I would die without you."

"And I, querida mia—"

She shook her head. "That's not what I meant to say at all, mi alma. It just came out when I opened my mouth."

"There is something else, then, sweetheart?"

143

"Si, Don Francisco awaits you in Don Augustin's counting room."

Juan was jarred by the news. He blinked at her soberly for half-a-minute before he licked his dry lips and spoke. "How? I didn't see him arrive."

"He has been here for an hour or so. His men are among the dancers—and everywhere." She smiled softly. "There are only twenty-eight, my lover."

The gray eyes grew dreamy. "Can a man collect twice, Señora, on the same debt?"

She answered in the same vein. "Not twice, darling of my heart. Twice a hundred times, and more, at his desire." She turned away, then. "But—go to him, my Juan. He isn't a patient man."

With a small gesture of affection he sought her hand and held it tightly for a moment, then turned and lost himself in the crowd, threading his way to the house.

Don Francisco Gardia was not, as Carmen had said and Juan knew, a patient man. When Juan entered the counting room he was standing with his back toward the door, watching the merriment through a window. Nor did he turn right away either, another indication of irritation at being kept waiting.

"Señor—a thousand apologies. I just this minute heard you were here."

Gardia turned slowly and smiled. It was a benign smile, but nevertheless there was annoyance—and something else in it, too. Something that struck Juan as being sadness and secrecy.

"Don Juan."

"A seat, Señor."

"Gracias. You—are a married man now?"

"Si."

"I hope in all sincerity that your own experiences in

144

that realm are more serene than were mine." The black eyes held to the gray ones for an instant, unblinkingly, then the expression changed slightly. "But—beyond offering my congratulations on this new status—that isn't why I am here."

Juan took the bull by the figurative horns. "Don Francisco, things have occurred to alter my outlook on riding with you." He saw the coldness coming up and made a futile gesture with his hands, then let them drop, inert, to his lap again.

There was no tactful way to say it at all. Just say it. Once before Francisco Gardia had shown that causes meant little to him. It was the ultimate that counted. Regardless of how Juan endeavored to justify his action, no explanation would completely suffice.

"I have changed my mind, Señor."

The silence was penetrating. Gardia was leaning back against the wall, impassive. The handsome face sagged with an inherent tiredness and the black eyes were blank.

"What can I say?"

Don Francisco spoke, then, suddenly, in a solemn tone. "You could tell me that our cause is a lost one, Señor, before we embark on it. I have met with this identical reply to my questions from no less than two-thirds of those who were to ride with us—with me."

"You don't see it that way?"

"Don Juan—evidently my line of reasoning is old-fashioned. I am convinced that no battle is decided until it has been fought. What, I ask you, can we determine, until we try? Nothing. It is the same here. I venture the belief—hope anyway—that those Californios south of us, won't have become defeated in their minds as you, and others have become, in our locale.

"Look you, Juan Martin," the big shoulders hunched over in earnestness, the large fists were clasped together intently, "there remains this Kearny who enters the territory from across the desert. He will be the crucial personality now. Oh, there are others, I admit, like this fool of a Stockton with his frightened navy who lies at San Diego, afraid of his shadow. But none of these dogs will move until this Kearny comes over the desert. Now then, caballero, I call your attention to a fact that can whip Kearny without much more than a little encouragement from Californio lances. Jornada de muerto." The big man's head nodded affirmatively twice, quickly.

"His men will be scarecrows and his horses will be half dead, if not completely so. After all, Don Juan, crossing that desert had cost the life of far more experienced travelers than these Americans. Do you see, then, that victory is within our grasp?"

Juan sighed, regarded Gardia gravely and wondered just how much of this he believed himself, and how much was recruiting talk.

"Don Francisco, when a man passes his word it should be binding. This is the first time in my life I have ever gone back on mine."

"Then why?"

"It's simple, to me. You may whip Kearny, I don't doubt for a moment, if the Californios put their united hearts into it, Señor, they can do it easily—readily. But there is more to the affair than this."

"Oh? Such as . . .?"

Juan shrugged and leaned back, watching Gardia's face. "There is a thing called destiny, Señor. It is highly probable that one of you, in California, have been in a position to see it objectively before."

146

"Destiny?" Don Francisco said, frowning his puzzlement. "How, destiny?"

"The United States has absorbed other areas of the continent. You are aware of this. America appears to me to be moving south and west now. Toward Mexico and California. It is, in my opinion, the destiny of this nation to swallow up the unprotected areas of the continent, and, while I'm neither in favor of this annexation of California, nor a war against Mexico, I tell you plainly, Señor, that it is preferable to having California taken over by foreign interests.

"Once you, yourself, told me that our loyalties are seriously divided. I spoke hastily then, out of resentment for anything that would change Alta California. On reflection I see how rash I was. Señor Gardia—nothing will stop an American acquisition of California. It is the manifest destiny of this eastern cousin of our's to do this. Moreover, I'm in favor of American acquisition, over foreign annexation.

"In other words, Señor, if I cannot see the possibility of victory for us at all then I think we should embrace the best alternative and make the most of it. Fighting for no better reason than because we want to fight, is folly. It'll not only cause us many enemies later, but may well cause a number of unnecessary deaths—on both sides— as well."

Francisco Gardia's expression wasn't as irate and indignant as Juan had expected it to be. "Well," he said dryly, "another disappointment met along the way, then, Don Juan. In a way, I can appreciate your beliefs, for, although I certainly don't share them, there is still a sprinkling of wisdom in them."

Gardia sat for a full minute saying nothing, then, very slowly, he reached inside the jacket he wore and withdrew a long, folded paper heavy with seals, and looked at it. "Don Juan—I will leave now. This paper— will you tell Don Augustin it is on his table?"

"Of course, Señor. Won't you stay for a little? There will be dancing later. Much food and amusement—"

"Thank you, no. With the reverses I've had in my own territory, I'll need all the time I can get in route to fill out the ranks before I arrive at the pueblo."

Juan wanted in the worst way to ask about Elena. There was no way under the sun he could do it though. They both arose. For a moment Francisco Gardia's melancholy eyes held to Juan's face, then dropped away. "Señor," he said softly, "adios."

The atmosphere in the counting room was heavy for a long time after Gardia had left. Juan sat back down, saw the letter lying on Augustin's table, and looked at it without really seeing it. His legs felt like leaky botas filled with warm water. Gradually, the shouts of the people outside drew his attention. The noise rose into a frenzied farewell, then the clatter of caballeros off to the wars, their horses thundering in a reckless, devil-may-care dash from the yard of San Diego Del Carmelo, made the air reverberate in his ears and he arose to watch the riders careen away over the range.

Don Augustin wasn't far from his table of wines when Juan found him. The old face was blushing a becoming rose color from the heat—and other things. "Señor?" he said, blinking up at Juan's face. "You look like an unpleasantness has taken you."

"I have felt less sorrow at times, Señor," Juan said dryly. "Don Francisco left a letter for you on your table and asked that I so inform you."

Augustin's eyes flashed an indignant fire. "Mother of God! These fools and their slips of paper. I warn you,

148

Juan—there can little good come from this new world we are embarking in, when everything is ordained on papers. Time was, son, when a man's mouth or an Indian's legs were sufficient to carry the most important of messages." Curiosity, too, had a part in the old Colonizer's make-up though. He sucked in his nether lip speculatively. "What do you suppose is in this accursed paper, Juan?"

"I have no idea, Señor."

"Well you told Don Francisco you weren't riding with him?"

"Si."

"His reaction, then?"

Juan shrugged. "Better than I anticipated. He—seemed abstracted some way, Don Augustin. He argued, of course, but it was very plain that his mind was a long way off."

"Seguro, he is that kind of a man. Not much given to clever arguments. He is, indeed a bull." Augustin nodded thoughtfully, then reached out and touched Juan's arm. "Come—let's see what is in this paper."

They went together, Juan walking slowly to allow full tolerance for his relation's exaggerated, slightly benumbed gait, and when they arrived in the counting room with the racket muted by the massive adobe walls and entering the room by its single unglazed window. Augustin peered down at the letter, picked it up, hefted it and passed it to Juan for study.

Juan read the letter twice, unbelieving, with a great suspicion forming in his mind. An obdurate growth that assumed prodigious size with each second that went by while he stood aghast, staring at the paper.

"Well," Augustin said irritably. "What is it? You look as though a fantasma—ghost—was lying there in your

149

hands—those hands." he added suddenly, looking at the bruised knuckles with wine inspired fascination, "which have such an incredible power. Come, then, what does it say?"

"It is a deed, Señor."

"Caramba! A deed? But I've bought nothing from Don Francisco!"

"Nevertheless, it is a deed to Rancho San Buenaventura, together with all its chattels."

"Now, in the name of God, what is this foolishness?"

Juan put the paper down on the desk without looking at Don Augustin or the letter. "You will own San Buenaventura and everything on it, Don Augustin, the day you have this—this paper recorded officially at Santa Barbara!"

Augustin's eyes were clearing a little in shock. Hi, mouth worked several times but no words came out. He glanced at Juan's face, saw the established look of pure horror on it, and swore an ancient oath as he reached for the paper, stared at it uncomprehending, then slowly put it down and, quite unconsciously, placed a heavy dagger kept as a paper weight on the thing. The action caught Juan's attention. He glanced down, saw the shiny blade resting athwart the paper and started violently, turned brusquely and strode out of the room with large, frantic steps that carried him beyond hearing of the astonished grunt that Don Augustin emitted, through the throngs of revelers and to the corrals where he hastily saddled a horse, unmindful of the noise about him, swung up and spurred out of the yard.

Although it was late in the year, the sun was hot and sparkling clear. Juan rode without seeing the beauty around him. He pushed his horse almost to its limit, then reined up suddenly when he topped a rolling land swell and spied a horseman riding in the same direction that he was, not more than a mile ahead. There was something familiar to the man's outline. He eased his sweaty animal down the far side of the ridge and kicked him out into an easy lope. It didn't take long to overtake the rider, who was going at a jog, obviously unaware that he was being followed.

"Mira, vaquero!"

The rider reined up and spun his horse. It was Hernando Vaz. Surprise showed even at that distance in his face. "Juan, what are you doing here?"

"The same as you, Hernan'. Going to San Buenaventura." Juan kneed his horse up beside the vaquero's animal. They went ahead then, in silent accord. He looked at the deep purple blemishes on his companion's face and was glad to see so much of the swelling had gone.

They rode in embarrassed silence for a way, then Hernando took his courage in his hands. "Juan—you are also going to ride with Gardia's force?" The black eyes went over Juan's unarmed state. "Where, then, are your weapons?"

"Hernan'—Don Francisco left San Buenaventura about daybreak this morning."

Vaz reined up quickly and shot a look of great disappointment and astonishment at Juan. "You—are certain of this?"

"Si, he was at San Diego Del Carmelo less than two hours ago, riding south with his men."

"Chihuahu!" Hernando's face grew bitter then, as He rode on, facing ahead, in silence.

"Hernan'—Don Francisco left a deed to Don Augustin for all of San Buenaventura. For everything; horses, buildings—everything."

Again the startled look appeared on Vaz's face. "But—why? What is there to this, Juan?"

151

"I don't know," Juan said quietly "That's why I'm riding over there. I fear—well—we'll be there shortly. Let's wait and see."

They were in the yard of Gardia's rancho before Hernando spun suddenly and stared at Juan. His features were twisted and frozen with a monstrous suspicion. He dismounted like a man in a trance, didn't even see the vaquero who took their horses, and went over close beside Juan who went toward the big house with only the barest acknowledgment of the nods he received from Rancho San Buenaventura's capataz—overseer.

The house was deathly quiet when they entered. Juan saw a dusky face peer at them and hailed the women who came forward with an unusual pallor and eyes the size of pesos. Blank, horrified eyes. They told Juan what he wanted to know in a sickening glance.

"Where is the Señora?" he asked in a dull voice.

Without another glance the servant turned and led them through the rooms until they came to the customary hallway leading to the smaller bedrooms and offices. She said nothing, only pointed and stepped aside with a furtive, fast movement of her right hand that sketched a hasty, irregular cross over her ample bosom.

Hernando stood perfectly still, caught up in the fear that emanated from the Indian woman, watching Juan shove past and stalk through the gloomy corridor, his immense spurs dragging with a somber musical accompaniment to his stride.

When Juan finally found the right door, opened it and stood in the well, his suspicions turned to fact. The dread was resolved and the horror was anti-climactic. It was a case of deducting a man's actions from his personality—plus his own justice, which every ranchero

152

meted out upon his domain with little interference from outside authorities.

There was little to show the agony. Elena Gardia was asleep. True, there was a pallor, a certain ethereal beauty that was unearthly, but mainly all the tensions, frustrations and violent passions were gone. At long last the beautiful woman had her repose, and no hint of the route her soul traveled—to Heaven, or—el tierra infierno—could be seen in the fine features, lax and firm and so, so dead.

He had no idea how long he stood there, looking down at Elena Gardia. It may have been moments or hours—days even—an eternity, before he entered the room, smelled the death in it, went over slowly and lifted the sheet. A small, triangular purple mark was in the golden flesh. It was apparent she had died as she slept in her bed, with one swift, merciful stroke of a long bladed poniard.

He couldn't help but think once, bitterly, that justice, after all, was a matter of interpretation. Her's was interpreted by a bear of a man to whom melancholy and resignation had become a part, but not commiseration nor forgiveness for continual transgressions. There was an overpowering sadness in Juan, but no anger against the hand that had killed her. A justifiable sentence had reached out and struck down this magnificent source of evil, and righteously too, for within her was the origin of all evil, the very root of destruction, like a malignancy, that would never cease bringing sorrow and suffering and death to others, until her heart was stilled.

He went back over to the door and stood there, looking up the corridor at Hernando. The vaquero's eyes were immense but he remained where he was, unwilling after all, to sacrifice his soul by a last look at the she-devil who had nearly cost him his life.

The Indian woman stared at him. This recalled the realities of the living to mind. He nodded to her. "Send the mayordomo to me."

"Here?" she said incredulously. "Señor—they know. All the vaqueros and laborers know. I—doubt if he will come here."

"Send him!" Juan said harshly, letting the annoyance he had always felt toward the Californios' fear of the unknown, and death in violence especially, show in his speech.

The woman turned abruptly and left the room. They were left alone, he and Hernando, staring at one another. The vaquero's eyes were glassy.

"Don Juan—"

"Si, she is dead."

"Ahhh!" Hernan' seemed to wilt a little. His eyes dropped to the floor and remained there while quiet words came out of his slack mouth. "Don Francisco, then—then—he—I thought it was this when we rode into the yard. It—was in the air, no?"

"Yes, I think so. It was also forming in his mind, Hernan', the morning of the duel. I saw it then and wondered what it was. Twice, now, lately, I have seen things and guessed wrong about them. It was there—I know it now, although I didn't understand it then." Hernando said nothing. He didn't appear even to hear. Juan spoke again. His voice had a soothing, sad sound to it. "There is a form of justice here, amigo. She was many things and, unfortunately, instinctive evil was one of them. Don Francisco was sick of killing men over her. He knew where the basis of all this anguish lay—and did away with it. May God have mercy on her soul, Hernando!"

154

"Ah—si, si, Don Juan. May she go with God." Hernando jerked to life then, his shoulders shook in spite of the effort he made to control them. He turned swiftly and went back through the house. Juan stood where he was, listening to the soft music of the huge spur rowels. He was still standing there when the overseer came in, poblano in hand, uneasy in the extreme and pale in the face.

"Señor?"

"You are the mayordomo, no?"

"Si, Señor. The capataz, Gonzalo Garces." The man made a slight, frantic, aggrieved motion with one hand, still holding the hat and curling its leather edge violently in his powerful hands.

"Mother of God, Señor! Why did this happen?"

Juan shrugged slightly "It has, Chollo Garces, that alone matters. Rancho San Buenaventura was deeded to Don Augustin Perez this morning by Don Francisco Gardia. This is for your information, vaquero. You will operate as you always have under Don Francisco. In time, of course, we of San Diego Del Carmelo will change things, here and there, but until that time, please do as you would do under normal circumstances. You comprehend, hombre?"

"Si, Señor. Every word. But—it can't be the same. You will understand, Señor."

Juan wanted to reach out and grasp the man's arm, to squeeze it and say something appropriate—but he didn't. He just nodded. "It is God's will—amigo. Adios."

The capataz turned finally, with dragging steps and lowered head. He went out of the house and Juan followed soon after.

Hernando was gone. Juan was relieved in a way. He

155

rode slowly back to San Diego Del Carmelo with twin sensations—one of huge sadness and melancholy, the other of relief. Not of callous relief, nor with the feelings of a man relieved of a load of guilt, but with relief that Elena Gardia's little devil was forever taken from the land.

✳✳✳

Time assuages all things. Memories remain always, truly, but poignancy softens them. At San Diego Del Carmelo, when the frosts were brittle on the ponds and the trees were like naked, supplicating fingers reaching toward leaden skies, two things occurred simultaneously. The first was of immediate importance. It reactivated the old rancho as nothing like it had done in over twenty years. Don Augustin drank with Juan and Hernando and his eyes, shaded lately with a mellowness of gloom and sorrow, were alight again.

"Hombres! This is the most excellent of all San Diego Del Carmelo wines. It has been saved for many years—since before any of you were born, in fact, for just such an occasion. Don Juan! Don Hernando! I offer this toast. May it be a boy!"

They drank silently with gratitude on their faces and in their hearts.

Later, that same day, a vaquero from the northern ranchos stopped by long enough to linger over a brief meal with the rancho folk. They ate and drank, then the rider beckoned the men aside, crossed himself and told them the news.

"Señors, Don Francisco Gardia of Rancho San Buenaventura—is dead."

156

Augustin and Hernando stared in shock. Juan felt differently. He had known, in a way—wondered more, perhaps—if this wouldn't have been Don Francisco's way.

"There was a battle far to the south. It was a foggy, accursed day, Señors. The place is called San Pasqual. We met this dog of a Kearny; routed him, in fact, and beat him to his knees."

"Don Francisco," Juan prompted the man.

"Si—yes. Don Francisco—with his huge bulk—lanced this Kearny. I saw the Yanqui's tunic rip with the strike, too, but Don Francisco didn't wheel and come back like the rest of us. He rode down the line of them, lancing Americanos like a devil—. Señors." The vaquero's shoulders rose and fell. "It was inevitable. He was sabered to death by a great circle of them. He and his big horse."

"Gracias, amigo," Juan said evenly, seeing the pain on Augustin's face. "I'll escort you to your horse."

When they were in the yard, Juan watched the man mount and looked into his face. "It—was a deliberate thing, was it not—Don Francisco's death?"

"Of a certainty, Don Juan. It could have been nothing else. Suicide. It ruined the morale of our lancers, too. A sad, brave thing. Well—Señor—I am indebted to you all. Adios."

Juan nodded. "Adios, vaquero, may God watch you on your return."

The man rode away in a brisk jog. Juan watched him disappear into the gray day. He stood alone, thinking how ironic it was that Don Francisco Gardia, by his own great bravery and destruction before the eyes of his men, had contributed by this same courage, in demoralizing,—thus aiding the defeat of his troops.

157

He was still standing like that when a soft voice called to him from what seemed milleniums away. He turned and saw Carmen's hand reaching out for him. Her black eyes were shining with an adoring luster.

"Juan, my soul—it—is all over, now? All of it?"

"Si, corazon, all of it. Don Francisco now, too, is departed."

She pulled at his fingers a little. "Come then, darling, we can both kneel together in this final prayer for Elena and Francisco Gardia."

He let her lead him back toward the house where one room was a small chapel. He watched her as she walked and said another prayer, less somber, for the Great Capataz to know that he, Don John Martin, was grateful and humble, both, for this infinite treasure of a wife.

We hope that you enjoyed reading this
Sagebrush Large Print Western.
If you would like to read more Sagebrush titles,
ask your librarian or contact the Publishers:

United States and Canada

Thomas T. Beeler, *Publisher*
Post Office Box 659
Hampton Falls, New Hampshire 03844-0659
(800) 251-8726

United Kingdom, Eire, and
the Republic of South Africa

Isis Publishing Ltd
7 Centremead
Osney Mead
Oxford OX2 0ES England
(01865) 250333

Australia and New Zealand

Australian Large Print Audio & Video P/L
17 Mohr Street
Tullamarine, Victoria, 3043, Australia
1 800 335 364